HARVE

A MAX BOUCHER

MYSTERY

BY TROY LAMBERT

This is a work of fiction, and geographic names and places have been changed, and any resemblance to real people or events is purely unintentional.

13 Digit ISBN: 978-0-9860309-7-0
10 Digit ISBN: 0-9860309-7-X

Dedication

To all those who believed in me and this work over the last few years when it seemed I might never write again.

Especially Jim and Rachel who remained faithful friends in the worst of times. Also, to Shannon, whose love helped me believe in myself again and reawakened my creative spirit.

In addition, this book is dedicated to my daughters Myndi and Valerie, and to my son Andrew for keeping me accountable when it came time to save myself.

And to my editors, beta readers, cover designer, and all those who worked tirelessly to make this book possible.

Finally, to Indie, my lab and best friend for over a decade before his passing, and to Houston, his predecessor. A dog truly is a man's best friend.

HARVESTED

Author's Note: Time

When you are a young writer, it seems impossible that you will ever have enough ideas to fill even one novel. As you write longer, it seems you will never run out. But occasionally time stops, life interrupts, and you feel like you are stuck, not for lack of ideas, but because you have no time, no method, to articulate them.

It happened to me. For three years, I wrote almost no fiction, and almost everything I wrote on a freelance basis was for someone else. Many of those things never even had my name on them.

Not that I regret any of them. They were all great writing practice, and it kept my mind and my research muscles limber. Freelance did, and still does pay the bills. But there was something missing inside me.

I've found it again, and now time seems to be racing forward. There are so many things I want to write, so many stories to get out of my head, and so little time to do it. Time. The thing we never seem to have enough of. There is no way to make more of it, no way to save what you did not use well for another day. When it is gone, it's gone.

So, thank you. For taking your time to read this book. I'm proud of every moment I spent writing it.

Table of Contents

Table of Contents

Part One: Dogs Gone

"All good is hard. All evil is easy. Dying, losing, cheating, and mediocrity is easy. Stay away from easy."

--Scott Alexander

HARVESTED

Chapter One

The Skylark died as he pulled into the space. The engine hadn't been tuned up since he had it rebuilt two years ago, and Max fully intended to get to it as soon as he had time.

Time. It felt odd, he thought, that the one thing he'd never had enough of before was the thing he still never had enough of now.

Before. A powerful word when it referred to the time you lost your entire family. Max had been a cop, and losing a family was not uncommon, when it was due to divorce or other tragedies related to the job.

That was not the case for Max. Max had lost his child to murder, his wife to kidnapping, and someone had killed his dog. His wife, Jenny was presumed dead by the Seattle Police Department, the FBI, and anyone else he'd been able to interest in investigating. Max knew better.

She was a missing person, an open case, and the reason he was walking into the stairway of a narrow building up to the apartment above his small office in Beacon Hill rather than into the police precinct. He'd left the force.

Max Boucher worked as a private investigator, with his own shingle, his own office, and his own stack of bills, including the mortgage on the house on Queen Anne Hill where he no longer lived but couldn't bear to sell. The moment he did, he would discover there was one more clue there he'd overlooked, one more thing he should've checked. Once it was gone, he wouldn't be able to.

It was the house where his daughter had been killed, his wife taken.

Max rarely turned down a client. Hell, he couldn't afford to. That meant sixty-hour weeks with little time to follow up on his wife's disappearance and who might have killed his family. So, Max Boucher did what every driven P.I. following up on a case of his own did. He went without sleep, and when he absolutely had to rest, he used the most common self-medication known to man.

He drank.

Max was otherwise healthy, at least physically. He didn't smoke, ran nearly every day, and somehow found time to visit the gym three times a week, time he spent mostly taking out his frustrations on a heavy bag. The bottle was his one downfall, and he didn't hide it. His hair, still department-short for convenience, was still as thick as it ever had been.

But the windows to his soul? Max avoided mirrors with astonishing success, because he didn't want to see his own eyes. They showed too much of his pain.

"Mr. Boucher?" A voice said from behind him.

He turned and saw a diminutive woman standing at the bottom of the stairs. "That's me," he said.

"Do you have a minute?"

He did but didn't know if this was how he wanted to use it. He was particularly thirsty, as his mind had been particularly active today. He'd seen a woman on the street who looked just like Jenny. Until he got within about twenty yards, and discovered she was shorter, with different colored eyes.

After three years, it still happened with too much regularity for his comfort.

"Maybe one," he answered. "What can I do for you?"

"I'd like to hire you," she said.

4

Max had just finished one case. His bills were pretty much caught up. His cupboard was full of groceries, and his liquor cabinet did not lack Scotch, even though it might not be entirely comprised of his favorites.

"I have kind of a full schedule at the moment," he lied. "Maybe you could come back tomorrow, and we could talk about it."

Max licked his lips. He could already taste the liquor, feel the burn in his throat and then belly. Maybe he'd be able to close his eyes. Rest maybe even sleep most of the night before his daughter's ghost woke him.

"Please, Mr. Boucher. A man named Tony referred me to you."

"Tony Delato?" Tony was his ex-partner.

"Yes sir. That's the one. He said you'd understand."

"Since Tony sent you, tell me what's on your mind. Not a husband thing, I hope."

"Nothing like that, Mr. Boucher. My dog is missing."

***

What does Tony think I am now, a pet detective? he thought. He'd reluctantly come back down the stairs, and sat with the woman in his office, him in a worn, second hand swivel chair he'd found on a corner bearing a big sign that said 'FREE.'

The woman sat in a well-used padded throne-like chair he'd found at a Goodwill store. The rest of the office held cheap furniture, including the scratched oak desk he sat behind, and a couch that hailed from 1976, upholstered in a delightful pea soup green. A painting on the wall depicted a velvet Elvis and hung at an awkward angle.

"How long has he been missing?" he asked, laptop open in front of him.

"She. About two weeks."

"What's her name?"

"Jennifer."

Max sucked a breath through his teeth. Jennifer. Jenny for short.

"Unusual name for a dog." He said out loud.

"Named after my mother," she said. "Are you okay?"

"Sure."

"You looked pale there for a second."

"Goose walked over my grave, I guess." Not the brightest thing to say, given the memories the name awakened.

The woman, who'd identified herself as Helen Ebbley, smiled thinly.

"What makes you think she didn't just run off?" Max asked, typing.

Helen looked around, decidedly uncomfortable. Max didn't blame her. If he'd walked into this office, he'd have doubts about its occupant as well.

Yet she stayed. Tony must have some influence on her.

The state of the office was the reason he conducted most of his client meetings at the coffee shop on the corner. At least there, he could offer something non-alcoholic to drink other than the putrid water from the tap in the corner.

"She wouldn't," was the simple answer, applied by dog owners and parents of teenage runaways the world over. He'd found seven missing teens in two years, something some considered heroic. He never confessed to recognizing three of them from porn flicks he'd seen, created right here in the city, and two of the others from undercover time he'd spent in vice.

"So, you checked all the obvious places," he stated. "Shelters, rescues, all that?"

"Yes sir."

"Please, Max is just fine."

"Of course, sir."

It was going to be a long night.

"Do you have a picture?"

"Several," Miss Ebbley said. A symptom of the times, she pulled out a tablet rather than an album, and tapped the screen.

A series of photos appeared. Max expected to see some kind of show dog, the kind folks usually set up rewards and paid private dicks to find. But it wasn't.

The dog was a large mutt. The meaty beast looked like she had at least some pit bull in her, and from comparison with the other objects in the photos, Max guessed her at around 100 pounds, probably thigh high on him.

Bigger than the dog he'd lost in the slaughter of his family. Thankfully, this one didn't look a thing like Houston.

"Anyone you know who'd want to steal her?" he asked after studying the pictures for a few moments.

"Not that I can think of, but there is something odd."

"Odd?"

"Yes sir. That's why Tony told me to come see you. There isn't much the Seattle police can do, or so he says, but several dogs have disappeared lately from the dog park where we go all the time."

"Several."

"A dozen I know of."

"The other owners, I assume they have looked in the usual places as well?"

"Every last one."

"You think there is a dog-napper on the loose, and you want me to find him?"

"Yes sir."

"Max."

"What?" she said, blinking.

"Max's my name. Not sir,"

"Yes—Max," she said, clearly experiencing pain from using his first name,

"My usual fee is—"

"We pooled our money. Will five thousand work as a retainer?"

To find some missing dogs? he thought.

"That would be a good start."

"Good, si—Max. I have set up a meeting with the other owners tomorrow afternoon at one. Can you be there?"

Max clicked the keys on his laptop, pretending to check his calendar. Really, he was checking his bank balance, thinking of how much healthier five g's would make it.

"I can be there," he said. "Where are we meeting?"

"Kinnear Park, of course," she said with a smile, handing him an address.

"Near the Olympic and 9th West entrance?" he asked. Queen Anne Hill. Not too far from his house.

His house in Queen Anne, where *It* happened.

"Are you okay, Max?" she asked.

"Fine," he said, standing to indicate the interview was over.

Picking up her purse, she stood to leave.

"Thanks, Mr. Boucher."

"You're welcome," he said.

Once he'd shown her out, he headed up the stairs. His sleep aid was waiting to be consumed, and suddenly he really needed it. Taking a case in Queen Anne? What was he thinking?

He skipped the rocks, and went for three fingers, straight. Five grand was what he was thinking.

He hoped it would be worth the pain.

Chapter Two

Max didn't hear a word she said at first.

This was the place.

Retired police dogs usually ended up with the officers who trained and handled them. But Houston's handler, an ex-Army MP from Texas, was killed in the line of duty. When Houston was retired, Max adopted him. He remembered the day.

"Samantha honey?" he'd said into the phone.

"Daddy?" she'd said in her four-year-old voice.

"Tell your mommy to bring you down to the park."

"The one where the dogs don't have to be on the lease?"

"The leash, honey. Yes, that's the one."

"How come daddy?"

"I have a surprise for you, pumpkin."

She'd wrapped her arms around the dog, and that was when Max knew he'd made the right call. She and Houston had been best of friends from that day on. He'd felt safer when he was gone with the dog in the house.

Until that day three years ago.

Samantha was dead. The dog had not been enough protection after all.

"Sir? Max? Did you hear me?"

"Sorry," he apologized. "I used to live close by and used to bring my daughter and our dog here."

"What happened?" Helen asked. Her smug look told him she assumed divorce, as nearly everyone did at first.

"I know you!" a voice from the right end of the group called out. "You're the cop whose wife and daughter were killed."

"Ex-cop. And my wife is missing," he answered quietly.

"Really? That's not what I read."

Max felt himself getting angry. "The papers don't always get it right."

"Sorry," the man said, dropping his head. "That's been a few years, right?"

Max stepped forward. "We aren't here to talk about my family," he said coldly. He spun on his heel.

"Good day, Miss Ebbley. Thanks for the offer, but I think I'll pass."

"Wait!" she said.

Max did. He wasn't sure why but told himself he needed the money. It was a lie and he knew it. It was about more than the money at this point.

This was his neighborhood, even though he didn't live here anymore.

"Fine," he said. A headache was building behind his eyes, and he knew the cure. But it was early, and the socially acceptable hour for that cure remained hours away.

"Thank you, Mr. Boucher," Helen said, slipping back into her more formal tone. She turned to the group. "Everyone line up. You can tell Mr. Boucher your stories, briefly. Please provide him with a picture of your dog, a few if you have some copies you can part with."

Max opened a laptop he'd brought with him. It, and his smart phone were his acquiescence to technology. Samantha had taught him.

"You have to get with the times, Dad," she'd said.

So, he'd learned to text, call, and even utilize modern devices, something uncommon among the detectives his age on the force. As much as they embraced forensics and other modern tools, many still took photos with film cameras, and wrote reports awkwardly, hunt and peck typing with two fingers.

Max was a fair typist, for a guy, and had even purchased, with great reluctance at first, a portable scanner. It worked well for him now, in his new line of work or at least a line of work that still felt new.

As he put his fingers on the keys, he remembered his daughter, and her teaching him.

"Home row."

"The internet."

Her sweet, sweet voice.

He swallowed.

"Okay, who's first?" he asked once he'd connected the scanner.

He could have brought all of them to his office, the shithole in the wall.

But then they would know he lived and worked in Beacon Hill. Many would wonder why, and some might even know he still owned his house here and ask why he didn't live in it.

He'd rather do it here as long as the typical Seattle gray skies did not start oozing rain. He sat for an hour, scanning pictures, typing in notes.

All of the stories were the same. They'd come to the park, let their dogs free.

All had been approached by someone asking for directions. Nice folks, they'd all given them.

And when they turned back after their conversation, their dogs had been gone.

There were no purebred pups in the group. Most were mutts, larger dogs, but none seemed like anything special.

Whoever did this was not a who, but a them. A team.

And it wasn't for a puppy mill, or some kind of breeding scheme. Otherwise, they would have taken papered animals. It wasn't for ransom either. No one had gotten any kind of demands.

Whoever was doing this had a different motive.

Now, more than the neighborhood, more than the money, Max was curious.

Finally, he'd been presented a case other than following a husband or wife, taking photos through hotel windows with a long lens, or planting bugs to catch a cheater.

It reminded him of his days on the force.

"Thank you all," he addressed them, once he had everything he needed. He looked down at his computer. Just in time. The battery sat at 10%. The scanner sucked juice. "Miss Ebbley will be my contact. I'll be in touch with her about the case regularly. If you have any questions, please pass them through her."

"Do you think you can find them?" one owner asked from somewhere in the cluster of people.

"I'll do my best," he answered.

Max already had an idea of how he might start, at least.

Each owner came by and shook his hand. Max offered them words of comfort, playing the part. The women paid him special attention, something he did not fully understand. A few even brushed their hands across his arms, making him uncomfortable.

As the line dwindled, and he was left alone with Miss Ebbley, Max relaxed a bit

"Let me take you to dinner," Helen said.

"No thanks," Max answered.

"Rain check?" she asked, winking at him.

"Sure," he said. *Did she just wink at me?* he thought.

Max decided to call Tony. After he made one stop while he was in the area.

He felt Helen's eyes on him as he walked away.

Shit, she has a crush on me, he thought as he got into the old Skylark, and fired it up. It idled roughly. *Great.*

He waved and backed out. The engine caught and died as he shifted into drive.

I really need that tune up.

He started the car again and headed for his home.

***

Max unlocked the door. There was no paper, no mail, there were no flyers on the knob.

The caution tape and crime scene markers had long ago been removed.

Other than that, the house remained exactly as it had been three years ago, minus the bodies.

In the entryway was the blood stain where Houston died, defending his family. The dog shit had been cleaned up, but everything else was the same.

Magazines were still scattered on the floor.

The kitchen had been preserved as well. Another long-dried blood stain marked where his daughter had sat at the table.

The pans were on the stove, where they had been. Max had cleaned them out himself, then put them back in the exact same position as the day of the murder.

The trail of dried blood spatters led to the back door.

Outside, Jenny was somewhere, alive he was sure.

A service came by to do the lawn and kept up outside appearances. But Max didn't let anyone inside, ever.

He didn't want anything disturbed.

Somewhere here might be the clue, the piece to the puzzle that would lead him to his wife.

Another similar crime occurred on the same night, and it too remained unsolved.

The other victim's husband moved on, accepting the line "presumed dead," and if he was honest, Max was jealous. He needed more closure, but until he saw a body...

A sound came from behind him. The click of the front door opening.

It had been two years since he lived here, but before that he'd been here for ten.

Max knew his house, and what every sound meant.

He drew his pistol.

Careful not to disturb anything he moved back toward the living room.

He could hear breathing on the other side of the door. He swore he could.

A couple footsteps echoed, like someone trying to be quiet. An almost inaudible grunt followed.

Max waited, ready.

Counted three. Burst through the door.

Raised his gun.

"Hi Max," the intruder said. "Glad to see you back on the job."

Chapter Three

"Jesus Tony," Max lowered his gun. "What the fuck are you doing here?"

"Checking up on you. Helen said you'd be in the area, and I bet on the fact you'd come here."

"Get off the couch, Tony. You know nothing in this house gets moved."

"When are you going to have it cleaned, Max? Move back in?"

"You know the answer. When I find Jenny."

"You can't go on like this." Tony crossed his legs, leaning back.

"Tony, I'm telling you to get off the couch. I'm only gonna ask nicely once."

"Then what, Max? You gonna shoot me? How would that work toward preserving your precious fucking crime scene?" His ex- partner's tone was angry, and his own rose with it.

"Did you come here just to lecture me? We've had this talk before, remember?"

"And it's been six months since I heard from you. Six months. Is that what our friendship means to you? Really?"

"You know that's not true."

"How do I know? Because you say so? What about what you do? Trudy would like to see you, you know."

Max's anger left as quickly as it had built. His shoulders sagged in resignation.

He thought back. His friend was right.

"I'm sorry," he said. Max looked around the room. "But can we talk somewhere else? Not here."

"Sure. How about Stonyville, over on Queen Anne?"

"Sounds good. I'll follow you over."

"No, hop in my car. I'll drive," Tony answered.

"Just like old times?" Max said.

"Yep," Tony answered, holding out his hand. Max helped him rise from the couch.

As the other man stood, Max inspected the piece of furniture. It appeared nothing had been disturbed, but what if there was a hair, a single piece of DNA, and it was fleeing the scene on Tony's suit right now?

There wasn't a thing he could do about that, was there?

He followed his friend out the front door, locking it behind them.

"You sure you don't want me to follow you?" Max asked again.

"No, I'll bring you back. But grab your laptop. I have something to show you."

Max blinked, wondering what his former partner had in mind, and then retrieved the computer and the wall charger from the front seat of his Skylark parked in the driveway. He made sure the door was locked as well and followed his friend to the beat-up police issue sedan at the curb.

Max couldn't be sure, but it seemed like the same car Tony had been driving three years ago, when he'd quit being a cop for good.

For the first time in ages, Max missed the job.

***

"I wanted to see you, but I have business to discuss too," Tony started once they were seated with coffee in hand.

Max's was black, Tony's a milky-sweet substance hardly resembling the original drink.

"Helen said you referred her to me."

"Figured you'd be perfect," Tony said, taking a large sip. "You know the neighborhood, and you love dogs."

"Yeah?" Max said, sensing more. "What else?"

"There's nothing I can do on this one yet, but these aren't the only folks missing dogs. You probably already figured this isn't a puppy mill. Frankly, I have no idea what it is."

"The dogs are mostly mutts. I have no guesses either, at least at this point."

"Okay. Pull out that fancy laptop you got. You still got your handy scanner?"

Max nodded, retrieving both. "I need to plug in, though. I met with the owners at Kinnear. Ran down my battery scanning pictures."

Tony grunted, and looked around.

Stonyville had not changed a lot in three years, but like any trendy coffee shop, it attracted a strange mix of patrons, from the in-and-out on their way to work business professionals in search of a pick me up to local women's clubs or the occasional writer, bent over a laptop tapping keys rapidly or surfing the web, whether for research or the one thing Max had not engaged in, social media.

Not that he hadn't thought about it. Crowdsourcing, something relatively new to him, was being used to find lost items, pets, and even to solve crimes. It didn't threaten to put him out of business, at least not the way he saw it. It did take some of the more mundane, less interesting cases off his plate. He was actually thankful for it.

He'd been mulling over ways to use it to his advantage.

But as a result of these surfers, in search of free Wi-Fi, there were power strips everywhere. Max stood and moved toward a pair of couches in one corner of the room, with a clear view of the door.

Tony followed. Once Max had the computer booted, he set it on a coffee table, and plugged in the scanner. Tony pulled a file from a case he carried.

"I can't let you have this, and I probably shouldn't show it to you, but you can look at it, and scan what you need."

"What is it?" Max opened the file.

Right up front was a photo of a man, standing in front of what appeared to be a large cargo ship. The second showed him in front of a warehouse. Behind that a blurry one showed the man in front of a local animal shelter, holding a puppy. The man was grinning.

"Who is that?" he asked.

Tony waved at him. "Keep going."

Max did, setting the photos aside. Behind them was a list. There were at least 100 single names on it, many of them common dog names. Next to each was an address.

As he looked them over, Tony set another file on the table. For the moment, Max ignored it.

Behind the long list was another sheet, a shorter list of names. Next to each of them was also an address, but in another column was a final word in all caps.

FOUND

He flipped through the rest of the pages quickly. Interviews with owners, photos clipped to some of the pages, others with written descriptions.

He set the file aside and looked at the second one.

A label on the front said, "Vet Records."

"Tony, I can't scan all of these here. I won't have time."

"I know. The department gathered this file, but we can't do a thing with it."

"I get it. The stories are all similar, but there isn't anything criminal, at least not that you can do anything about."

"Right."

"And you think of me?"

"The owners, at least the ones in Queen Anne, are willing to pay. There are rewards out for some of the other dogs as well. Figured you could use the money."

"Who's the oriental guy?"

"A member of the Chijon family, Korean mob, oddly enough."

"Korean mob? What the hell does he have to do with this?"

"We don't know. He has been very active in dog rescues and shelters in the area. Very benevolent. Of course, we looked for a motive."

"Other than a legit tax shelter, appearing to be a good guy, or money laundering?"

"Besides that. Because he takes dogs, and promises to find them homes, get them adopted."

"Rescues and dogs from shelters?"

"Yeah. Only the dogs are never seen again. There are no records of the adoptions. Many rescues cut him off, and he can't take dogs from local shelters any more until he provides proof of where they are going."

"Let me guess. The dog disappearances started when they stopped accepting his generosity."

"Yep. And another thing. Strays are down, at least the medium to large type. Guy rarely took small dogs."

"Another odd coincidence. What does your gut say?"

"I'm puzzled. I thought maybe he was using them to train dog fighters. You know, practice partners. But he doesn't focus on the perceived aggressive breeds, or younger dogs. There seems to be no pattern, no preferred breed. In fact, most of the disappearances are mutts."

"Why do you think that is?"

"You take breeds, you draw attention. Mutts disappear all the time."

"You think he is taking the dogs, but you have no idea why?"

"That's about it."

"What are you sending me into, Tony?"

"I have no clue. None at all."

"I need to scan all this."

"Trudy will be delighted."

"About what?"

"That you are coming to dinner at our house, so you have time before I have to get this back tomorrow."

"You are a pain in my ass, you know that, right?" Max said.

"Right back at you," Tony said. He gathered the files as Max packed his computer gear into his bag.

The door to the coffee shop slammed open, the bell dinged loudly, and Max looked up.

A shot rang out. A blond headed, long haired young man in tattered clothes pointed a small pistol at the barista.

"Give me the money from the register, and no one gets hurt!" he shouted.

Just like a fucking movie, Max thought, and sighed, reaching for his gun at the same time Tony reached for his.

***

"Get down!" the thief screamed.

Bloodshot eyes darted around the room, looking for movement.

Max exchanged a glance with Tony, keeping his pistol hidden.

"Nobody do anything stupid!"

The barista had the register open, and was pulling out bills and coins, stuffing them in the cloth Trader Joe's bag the robber had generously provided.

Max took a quick survey of the room. Hands were on tables, patrons looking at each other in confusion. He saw at least two cell phones setting next to hands and assumed 9-1-1 had already been called.

Tony nudged him and nodded, apparently seeing the same thing. The cops were on their way, and tangling with a crazy, probably high robber was not top on the list of smart things to do.

What a mess.

The cashier handed the bag back, closed. The thief yanked it open and looked inside.

"Is that it?" he yelled. "There has to be more." His gaze darted side to side, landing on Max.

"You!" he said. "Get up. Grab everyone's wallets, jewelry, whatever. Put them in this." The robber grabbed a 'Reduce, Reuse, Recycle' shopping bag from a rack by the door that bore the slogan "Stonyville cares."

Max stood slowly, shoving his pistol down between the couch cushions to hide it from the angry kid.

Tony shot him a look.

Don't, it said.

Too late. Max was angry. This shithead was obviously an amateur, but either way, crime was crime, and dead was dead.

Taking money was one thing. But the way this punk was waving the pistol around, he might shoot someone any minute, probably accidentally.

Max smiled as he approached, reaching for the bag.

"What you grinning at?" the thief shouted into his face.

"You," Max said. He grabbed the bag, slid the handles down along the punk's wrist, and twisted them, trapping his hand. He pulled the kid toward him.

Up close, he could smell alcohol and see faded bruises under his eyes. He'd try to be as gentle as possible.

As expected, the punk brought the gun up, but Max was too close for him to use it effectively. With his free hand, Max grabbed the thief's other wrist, and applied pressure. He could feel the bones grind together.

This kid is thin and weak, he thought as he twisted. Breaking his arm would be way too easy.

The gun clattered to the floor, and in a second Tony was beside him.

His ex-partner scooped up the weapon, pulled cuffs from his belt in one smooth motion. Max released the handles of the bag, and Tony cuffed the perp.

The place erupted in applause.

An oriental man walked up from behind their captive, watching as Tony spun him around, pulled over a chair, and sat him in it. Sirens rose from the corner.

The new arrival picked up the bag of cash and handed it back to the cashier.

"Nice job you two," he said with a slight trace of an accent. "Are you cops?"

The thief was crying, and clearly no longer a threat. Tony took out his badge. "I am."

"I used to be," Max said, holding out his hand. "Now I'm a P.I."

"Like Magnum?" the other man asked, taking the offered hand to shake.

"Not quite that glamorous," Max answered. The handshake was light, but there was hidden strength in his grip. "You are?"

"Myung Yong," he replied. "I own a restaurant nearby."

"Pleased to meet you," he answered. "Max Boucher."

"Quite the name, Mr. Boucher."

"Max, please."

"Maybe I see you around?" His accent was suddenly more pronounced.

"Sure," Max said. Uniforms were coming through the front door, and Tony was gesturing to them. "Stick around. These guys are going to want statements from all the witnesses."

The oriental man nodded and bowed slightly.

Max turned his back on him, surveying the chaos.

"Mr. Boucher?" a uniform asked.

"That's me."

"Detective Delato says you saved the day."

"Don't know about that," Max said.

"Well, either way I need to get your statement. Can you follow me please?"

Max did. He knew the drill.

He surveyed the crowd as he went, saw the uniforms talking to all of the patrons. Some gestured toward him, a couple waved. Some appeared shaken, understandably so.

Max looked for the oriental man among them but didn't see him.

He was gone.

HARVESTED

Chapter Four

"This supper is great, Trudy." Max sipped the wine, not something he was usually into, and rolled more pasta onto his fork. The smell of garlic bread made him long for another piece.

"Thanks Max," she said. Her pale skin and dark hair belied her Italian descent. Her cooking solidified the image. "How have you been?"

"Not bad, all things considered."

"We miss having you around." He knew she genuinely did, and he had to admit to himself that he missed her too. Her statement was not something Tony had put her up to.

"I'll do better," he said, hoping he meant it. He really intended to, but time just seemed to slip away.

"What are you working on?" she asked.

Tony cleared his throat.

"What?" she said. "He isn't a cop anymore, talking out of school."

"Still..." Tony trailed off.

"It's fine," Max said. "I don't mind at all. I'm actually working on something Tony referred me. A dognapping."

"Dognapping? Really?"

"It seems a bit larger than that."

"Enough business." Tony shot her a look, and Trudy looked down at her hands. "We want to hear about you Max."

"Yes," Trudy said quickly. "Are you still living in Beacon Hill? Beside that place..."

"Shorty's," Max answered. "Yep." He knew where this was going and didn't like it at all.

"You seeing anyone?" she asked. From his side of the table, Tony hissed.

Max just shook his head.

Tony growled.

"What, it's been three years is all." Trudy turned to Max. "You are easy on the eyes. I know at least half a dozen women—"

"Trudy!" Tony cut her off.

"You think about cleaning the house up? Selling it, maybe?" she said nervously.

Max shook his head again, feeling ashamed. "Can we not talk about this?" he asked.

Trudy nodded. "I'll go get the dessert." She turned away from the table, but not before he saw the tears in her eyes.

When she was gone, Tony looked at him. "She does care you know."

"I know," Max said.

"She's worried about you."

"Me too sometimes."

"I hate to say she's right, but you do need to move on, Max."

"I know."

"You should talk to someone."

"A shrink? Who?"

"Hell, I don't know. Maybe the department has somebody. You want me to ask around?"

"Sure. I guess it can't hurt."

Max knew if he didn't say yes, he'd never hear the end of it. He had no intention of calling anyone. Hell, there was no way he had time, let alone money. The department had tried to get him to go before he left. Of course, he hadn't, although he'd faked it a few times to go to the bar. Or back to his house, for another look at the crime scene. Looks that sometimes took a number of hours.

The same as the look he'd planned this afternoon, just to be sure.

The one Tony had interrupted.

Trudy returned with plates holding large pieces of chocolate cake. "What are you boys talking about?"

"Max agreed to see someone," Tony said. "Professionally," he added when her face lit up.

"Oh, good," she said. "Do you have someone in mind?"

"Thought I'd ask around the department," Tony answered.

"I know someone," she said.

Tony groaned as Max said, "Really?"

"Yeah, let me get her card." She set down the cake in front of each of them and disappeared.

"I hope she isn't just setting you up, Max."

"Me too," he said.

Just then, a knock came at the door.

"You expecting anyone?" Max asked.

"Nope." They both got up, Tony taking the lead. He looked out the peep hole.

"Shit!" he said and yanked open the door.

On the porch sat a brown paper bag, on fire. It smelled like burning dog shit.

"Trudy bring water!" he shouted.

Max smiled. At least his friend hadn't tried to stomp it out.

Trudy came running out with a pitcher.

"Damn kids," Tony said. "Happens a couple times a month."

Max laughed but turned to look at Trudy. She was pale with fear.

"What's wrong?" he asked.

She pointed at the door.

Max looked and saw a piece of paper. It was stapled to what appeared to be a dog's ear.

The ear had a hole in it and had been hung with brown twine from a hook that had held a Christmas wreath the year before.

"Every dog has its day," the note read. It was neatly written on yellow lined paper with something brownish.

Without testing it, Max suspected it was blood.

Probably dog blood.

"Call the station," Tony barked.

"No," Max said. "Whoever did this is watching. And wanted to scare me. I'll handle it."

"I can't let you. This isn't just dog stealing any more. This is..." Tony trailed off.

"Is what?" Max said. "A really sick prank? The department will look at this, put a guy on it for a day or two, and then what?"

Tony nodded. "Fine. You're right. What do you want to do?"

"Let's get a picture before we move anything."

"Then?"

"I need to get the rest of those files scanned. Someone doesn't like me looking at this."

"Fine."

"I'll put on coffee," Trudy said.

"Good." Max sighed. It was going to be a long night. Maybe he could find some self-medication in Tony's cabinet.

* * *

At 4 a.m., Max crashed into Tony's guest bed with a gigantic headache.

He had a case file, full of nothing and a note he was sure was clean of fingerprints or anything else.

He also had a dog ear that could belong to any one of the half-dozen missing mutts, at least the most recent ones. Or to one taken long before. Or might not belong to any of them at all and could have come from anywhere. In fact, Tony said the flaming poop incidents happened often. It could just be a coincidence, but those were something Max didn't believe in.

Contrary to TV and movies, labs who could do DNA testing were both busy and rare. He could have had someone analyze the blood on the note and the ear, see if they were from the same dog, see if he could make an identification. All stuff a TV dick with unlimited money might have done. To what purpose?

No, this one, like many cases, would be solved with some solid detective work, but the immediate missing piece was the one that had been nagging at him since Helen Ebbley had walked into his office.

What was the motive? Who benefited from kidnapping mutts?

The notes on the member of the Chijon family raised more questions than it did answers. How did he benefit? Where was the profit?

These thoughts all tumbled through his mind as he closed his eyes. When he next opened them, the clock said 10:30 a.m.

He glanced at his phone, laying where he'd plugged it on the nightstand before he went to bed.

Six text messages, a dozen e-mails, and two voice mails.

Swiped the screen. Two missed calls from Miss Helen Ebbley.

Entered his voice mail password and hit play.

The first one was a second of silence, followed by "For the love of God!"

The second pleaded politely: "Call me back, please sir. Another dog disappeared. Thank you." There was a short pause, and then, "Where is he?"

The time stamp of the call read 8:37. Damn. Two hours. Leaving the texts and e-mails until later, he called her back.

"Miss Ebbley?" he asked when she answered.

"Yes, Max, where have you been?"

"Sorry, I was up late working on the case. I just woke up."

"Do you have anything new?" she asked.

"I have more information. But nothing to report. Your voice mail said there was another dog missing?"

"Yes. Just this morning. Can you meet me at the dog park?"

"Anything different this time?

"Maybe. We might have a witness."

Max hesitated. Time across town, plus he needed a shower, even if he didn't have another set of clothes.

"I'll meet you in 45 minutes," he said.

"Great!" she said. "See you there."

He ended the call. Looked at the texts. One from Tony.

"Had to go to work, see you soon."

The others were from an unknown number. Both were blank.

He shrugged. Found the e-mails unimportant, mostly junk.

He ducked out into the hall.

"Good morning," Trudy said from the bathroom.

"Hey there," he said. "Can I get a shower, and a lift to my car?"

"Sure," she said, tousling her hair one more time and moving out of the way. "You need clothes?"

"I'll be fine," he said. Once she shut the door, he stripped and got under the water. God, it felt good to be in this house again.

And busy.

He smiled as he scrubbed his scalp. Despite little sleep, he felt pretty good this morning.

***

Max's stomach growled.

He meant to grab a donut but had not. Instead, he'd only grabbed coffee, and rushed over.

A distraught older woman stood next to Helen, dabbing her eyes with a silk kerchief.

As Max shut off the ignition, the engine chugged, and took a moment to come to a halt. The need for a tune up became more urgent every day.

He'd hardly managed to get out the door when the woman confronted him.

"Are you the detective?" she asked, her voice clearly strained.

"I am," he replied. "Max Boucher." He held out his hand.

She left his hand hanging in midair. "Can you find my boy?" she asked.

"I will certainly try." Max remembered the ear but didn't want to add to her distress.

"Here is his picture," she said, shoving it into his hand.

The photo showed a large mutt, likely some kind of heeler mix. Triangular, pointy ear...

Ear. Singular. A bandage decorated the dog's head on one side.

"When was this taken?" he asked.

"What's wrong?" she asked.

Max composed his face, with some difficulty.

"I just want to make sure this is the most recent picture we have, that's all."

"Well, Jeffrey is a trouble maker sometimes. Day before yesterday he wandered off into the bushes over there, and I heard fighting. Of course, I rushed over, but when he came out, he was missing an ear."

'Did you see what did this to him?" he pointed at the picture. He had almost said who.

"No, but I took him to the vet, and she said it must have been another dog, at least she thought so. I even came back and tried to find the ear but couldn't. Is this relevant to finding him, Mr. Boucher?"

"It's Max. And maybe."

"Don't worry," Helen said, sliding up next to him, and slipping her arm into his. "Max knows what he's doing. He used to be a cop."

The woman's face blanched. "You're the one. The one whose wife..." she stopped. "I'm sorry."

A slight headache started behind Max's eyes. Did everyone in this goddamn neighborhood know him?

"It's fine," he said. "Can you show me where he was...injured?"

"Sure," she said.

Uncomfortable with Helen so close, Max disentangled himself from her, and followed the woman. Helen walked beside him.

"You said something about a witness?" he asked as they made their way across the open, grassy area.

"Yes. She went home, but we can swing by and I'll introduce you after this."

"Thanks," he said.

They followed the distraught owner in silence.

"Right here," she said.

A high set of bushes fronted a small grove of larger trees. Max stepped between them.

Inside, he found a clearing. One patch of ground was darker than the rest, and he knelt for a closer look.

The dirt had a reddish tint, and although he could not be sure, he thought it was blood. He took a small plastic bag from his pocket, turned it inside out, and used it to grab some of the darkened soil without getting it on his hands.

On one of the branches were a couple of what appeared to be canine hairs.

He retrieved them using a separate bag, with no real idea why. It wasn't like he could have them tested.

Something caught his eye, ahead and to the left. White cloth contrasted with the green of the leaves and branches. Slowly he stood, moving forward.

Max spread the branches aside, and in front of him was a white sheet. The bottom was splattered with red, soil stuck to where it appeared to be wet.

A folded note sat on the top. On the outside, it read simply "Boucher."

He should have gloves. But he didn't run into this type of thing much as a P.I. Reaching into his other pocket, Max removed another plastic sandwich bag and used it to pick up the piece of paper and flip it open.

"A doggone shame," he read. Max set the note carefully aside.

He looked at the bundle. Peeling back one corner, he saw fur. Opening it further, using the bag as a glove, he saw blood. Then one eye with an open wound above it, then another, and a single ear. The sticky sweet smell of fresh blood mixed with the odor of sweaty dog.

A dog lay in the sheet, a bandage around his middle. Whatever wound it covered appeared to have bled profusely.

Jeffrey, unless Max missed his bet.

He exited the bushes, calling out to Helen.

"Did you find something?"

"Yes, ma'am," he said, trying to remain calm. "Do you have an emergency vet's number? A local one? I'm going to need some help here."

"What is it?" Helen asked.

"Jeffrey, and he's hurt," Max said. Jeffrey's owner stood only a few feet away.

"My God!" she said. "Jeffrey!"

"Ma'am," Max said, and caught her arm. "Don't—"

"I've got to see him."

"Not like this. Let me get him the help he needs."

"No," she said, shaking her hand loose. She rushed between the stand of bushes.

Max followed, but he was too late. He heard sobbing.

Unsure what else to do, he swiped his phone open and hit a speed dial three years old.

"Delato here."

"Hey Tony."

"Max! Did you get up okay this morning? Did Trudy feed you before you could rush off?"

Max's stomach growled, despite the scene he was looking at.

A woman, kneeling in a sheet filled with her dog's blood. The dog, clearly in pain, licking his lips, eyes sorrowful.

Helen appeared, kneeling next to her friend.

"No, listen Tony."

"She'll-"

"Tony, one of the dogs has been found."

"Really? That's great Max."

"He's hurt Tony. We have an emergency vet on the way, at least I think so. Can you spare me a couple of techs, at least to gather some evidence?"

"Let me see what I can do. You know we're stretched thin Max."

"Call me back."

Boucher ended the call and went over to the ladies. "Is the vet on the way?"

"They don't have pet ambulances, Max. She said she would call animal control."

Max looked down at the dog. "Do either of you have a car here?"

Both women shook their heads. "We live a few blocks away. We always walk."

"Did you go home after your—after Jeffrey went missing?"

"Just to call you, and get Helen," the owner explained.

Behind them, Helen was examining the bandages, tears standing in her eyes. "We need to get him somewhere, Max."

Max thought of his car. The exterior might be getting a little beat up, the motor, rebuilt just a couple years ago might be in need of a tune up, but the interior was pristine.

There was a blanket in the trunk, but he couldn't put the dog in the trunk, could he?

He looked at the ladies. No, probably not.

"Stay with him. I'll be right back."

Max went to get his Skylark from the parking area. He could pull it up on the concrete paths, even the grass if he had to, get a little closer.

He guessed he would play pet ambulance this one time.

HARVESTED

Chapter Five

The blanket worked just fine when combined with the sheet but getting the dog in the back seat proved impossible. A two door was forever impractical if you had pets or kids.

That's what Jenny's car had been for, before she disappeared.

But he leaned the driver's seat forward enough for Helen and the dog owner, now introduced simply as Susan, to squeeze into the back seat. Both women had mud on the bottom of their shoes.

Susan slipped getting in, leaving a muddy hand print on the side of his driver's seat.

Max cringed but said nothing.

The dog whimpered, but he took that as a good sign. Dead dogs didn't make noise, something Max knew all too well.

"Where to?"

The ladies directed him through the streets to a clinic he was vaguely familiar with from his years of living here. It was not Houston's vet, but one he had driven by from time to time.

He pulled around back per their instructions and parked near a rear entrance.

Once he had freed the women from his now filthy back seat, Susan rushed inside. Two people in what looked like nurse's scrubs followed her out the door, wheeling a gurney. One of the two was a large man, the size of a college linebacker. The other was his polar opposite, a short, thin blonde in her early twenties.

"The doctor is prepping now," the big man rumbled.

"Susan?" Helen asked.

"I'll wait here."

"How will you get home?"

"I'll figure out a way."

"We'll make sure she is taken care of," the small woman said.

"Do you want me to bring you some clothes?"

Max studied both women. Fashionable clothing was now clearly ruined, covered in blood and mud.

"No, I'll be fine," Susan said.

The three of them disappeared inside, leaving Max alone with Helen.

"Give me a minute with her, Max. Then can you take me home?"

He looked sorrowfully at the interior of his car. Not much more harm could be done.

"Sure," he said aloud.

As Helen walked inside, Max's phone chirped.

"Boucher," he answered.

"We need to take this case back, Max."

"Tony. What do you mean?"

"This isn't just dognapping any more. There are threats. Animal cruelty. Jesus Max, there is blood all over this scene."

"I know, Tony, but I am at the vet's now. The dog seems like he'll probably make it."

"How would you know?"

"Well, he didn't croak on the way over. He was whimpering. I figured that was a good sign. I do know a bit about them."

"Sorry Max. I know…I mean…"

"It's fine Tony. Just answer one question. How much time can you dedicate to this?"

"Not really my department Max. There's no major crime here. Until there is, I can't run the case. But this is too big for you to handle alone."

"Really Tony? First you send the case to me, then you want me to leave it alone."

"Look, Max, you know they won't put the best men on this. They can't. No overtime either. You know how the budgets go. There's no extra money. I'm not even sure what crime this is. But there is more to this than meets the eye."

"You're asking me to back off?"

"Yes. There's clearly some danger. And over what? Some missing mutts? It's not worth it."

"I'm getting paid to look into it, and I plan to do just that."

"That's your right. I'm just advising you against it."

"You know I can't quit something like this, Tony."

"I said my piece."

"What now?"

"Let me know what the vet says about this—Jeffery did you say his name was?"

"Yes."

"Maybe I can get the animal crimes division to widen the investigation."

"Fine. I'll share whatever I get. I'll call you later."

Helen walked back out as he hung up. "Let's get you home," he said. "I'm going to need your clothes."

Her red rimmed eyes widened.

"For evidence," he clarified.

She sniffed and nodded. Max sighed in resignation as she slid into the already soiled passenger seat.

He turned the key, and the Skylark sputtered to life.

Tune up. Interior detail. Both soon, he promised himself.

"Where to?" he asked. The way things were going, he wasn't surprised at all when their route led him right past his home.

Maybe I'll stop by on my way back to the office, he thought. Just for a few minutes. Make sure everything is still in place.

A couple blocks later, they reached Helen's house. He locked the Skylark but left the windows down just a crack to let some of the smell out at least.

He felt like he was being watched as he followed Helen to her door. As she turned the key and opened it, his stomach growled loudly.

***

A matter of moments after they were inside, he heard the shower running.

He sighed. It was going to be a long afternoon. His stomach growled again, reminding him he'd skipped breakfast.

To his surprise, the shower shut off only a few minutes later. Helen reappeared, towel around her head, wearing a robe. Her soiled clothes were in a clear garbage bag.

"Here you are Mr. Boucher." She smiled, looking him over.

His stomach gurgled, louder this time.

"Can I interest you in some lunch?"

"That would be wonderful," he said. "Get dressed, and we'll grab a bite somewhere close by."

"No bother at all. I'll be happy to make something for you here."

"I'd hate to trouble you," he mumbled, but could tell his protest was fruitless.

"No bother at all. Come in the kitchen, and we can talk while I whip up something."

"I really should get going—"

"Come on," she cut him off. "Join me. You'll waste away if I don't get some food into you soon." The shower had turned her into a different woman than the one he'd found at the crime scene.

Max followed her into her kitchen, reluctant. There was a table to the side in a small breakfast nook, and he took a seat.

Her eyes were still red from tears, and although she tried to hide it, Helen was still clearly shaken. She bustled about, grabbing ingredients from the fridge and the cupboards, arranging them on the counter.

Max pulled his phone out of his pocket and swiped to check his email. A notification told him the power bill was due, only $43. He kept the heat quite low in the house nearby, and certainly no one was turning lights on and off.

In reality, he was hiding from his hostess. The knowledge she was naked under the short robe, facts revealed from time to time by her careless movements, made him uncomfortable.

He ran his fingers over his wedding ring.

Well-meaning women had approached him. But he'd been careful to avoid them in this type of situation, alone in their homes.

He felt trapped, the kitchen much too warm.

Standing, he broke the now awkward silence. "I think I'm going to step out for some air."

Before he could protest, she was in his arms, sobbing into his chest.

"Oh, Max, this is all so horrible."

He put his arms around her in a clumsy embrace. Anywhere his hands touched felt wrong.

The smell of her shampoo, a citrus something, filled his nostrils and his shirt was soon damp with her tears.

On the stove, a pot bubbled, filled with pasta. A wooden spoon rested across the rim.

Her head turned, and he felt her lips move against his chest. Against his will, his body reacted.

Turning her face up to him, she smiled, blinking away the tears. "You're an amazing man," she said. Her hands moved up his back, and she pressed closer.

He could feel her body against his and knew she could feel his as well.

"I can't, Helen." He felt his face redden, and he tried to push away. She held him in place.

"Don't worry, Max," she said. "I've heard about your wife. I have no desire to tempt you to do anything you don't want to. But if you were to want—something, anything at all, there would be no condemnation here."

"I think—"

"Or need for commitment," she finished quickly. "But no pressure. If not now, you know where to find me."

"I think it's best if we concentrate on the case," Max said, finally able to break free.

"Fine," she said, clearly disappointed. "Will you excuse me for a moment?"

As she turned to leave, she gestured at the sauce on the stove. "There's a spoon next to that pan. Stir, please."

Max stood and did as he was told. Within moments she returned, fully clothed, though alluringly.

You're crazy Max, he thought, but passed her the spoon without comment.

"So, the case?" she began, avoiding her earlier flirtations.

"Yes. Earlier, you mentioned a witness?" Max was pleased to find his voice steady and his earlier excitement fading.

"Oh dear. In all the excitement, I nearly forgot poor Alice."

"Alice?"

"She may not be the most reliable," she apologized. "But she's all we have."

"Do you think we can see her after lunch? I also need to go talk to the vet, check on Jeffery, and see what she found."

"We should be able to. Alice doesn't go out much, unless she is at the dog park. I'll take you over."

"Sounds fine," Max said. As they talked normally, his discomfort faded. A couple of times Helen paused to do something on her phone, texting he assumed.

With a flourish of small talk and clattering pans, Helen finished her creation, and set a plate in front of him. On it rested a red sauce of some sort, containing mushrooms and peppers, presented on a bed of swirled pasta. A second plate, set to one side, contained a small but delightful looking salad.

"This looks fantastic," he said. Max was no stranger to the kitchen but had not cooked since Jenny had been—gone. It seemed pointless to cook for himself.

Helen smiled. They made small talk as they ate, her taking seductive liberties with her food, attempting to allure him into more personal conversation with her questions.

Or so Max imagined. He deflected her inquiries but smiled at her efforts.

Once the dishes were cleared, he asked if she would like to ride with him to meet Alice.

"No need," she said.

The doorbell rang, and she rushed from the room.

***

Max followed, and when Alice entered, he could not help but feel he was being set up. Again.

She was gorgeous, another dark-haired woman who appeared to be of Italian descent. Her eyes were brilliant emerald green, contrasting perfectly with her milky white skin.

She wore spiked heels, and tight capris with a garishly large belt. Her blouse was conservative, but open from her throat to deep inside her generous cleavage.

Max tried not to stare or make it obvious he was admiring her.

Her Pomeranian made it easier. As his gaze traveled north, the dog yipped and barked at him, and would not stop.

"Oh, Felicia, he is a good man," she cooed. The dog refused her comfort.

"I'm—"

"You're Max Boucher. Helen has told me *all* about you."

Her emphasis on the word "all" made him uncomfortable yet again. He had no idea why suddenly he was being bombarded with women: willing, single, clearly hungry women around what he perceived to be a serious case. He wanted to leave right then, yet another part of him was curious. She might actually have seen something.

Max reached out to pet the dog, but it nipped at his fingers.

"Felicia," she chided. "Be a good girl."

The dog appeared determined to do just the opposite.

"Here," Helen said. "I'll put her in the back room while we talk."

"Would you dear?" Alice smiled. Helen took the dog and disappeared.

She moved to the couch in a house she was clearly familiar with and sat, patting the cushion next to her.

Max moved to a chair across from her instead. He took a notebook and pen from his pocket.

Alice pouted for a second at his seating choice, but then smiled. She sat forward, elbows on her knees.

"What do you want to ask, Mr. Boucher?"

"Perhaps you could just tell me what you saw this morning."

"Oh, yeah. That." She seemed to just now recall why they were here.

"Yes. Just start at the beginning. Any detail could be vital."

"Well, this might sound crazy."

"Let me decide that," Max said, his patience growing thin. He felt like Helen was parading him in front of her single friends almost like a spectacle. He really wanted to get on with the case. The clock on the wall already read 2:30. There was no way he'd have time to stop by his house and make it to the vet as well. Not before five.

He wanted to make that visit today.

"Well, I saw a van."

"A van?"

"The delivery kind. Like restaurants use?"

"Did you see a license plate?"

"No. Nothing like that." Alice giggled, and just then Helen came back into the room. She looked like she'd been crying again.

Jesus, Max thought. *What now?*

"I did see writing on the side," she said.

"Writing?"

"Yeah, but it was a word that didn't make sense. And then some symbols. You know, like Japanese or Chinese letters?"

"Could it have been Korean?" Max asked, and then felt stupid for doing so. There was no way she would know the difference.

"Well, could have been," she said.

"Do you remember any of the words?"

"One looked like young, only spelled wrong. Like Y-O-N-G." Alice pronounced each letter carefully.

"What makes you think the van had anything to do with it?"

"Well, because. One guy went into the cafe, you know, across the street? But as he was leaving, another man came running across the park."

"Across the park?"

"Yeah, and he was carrying a bag."

"Large or small?"

"Large. It looked heavy."

"What did he look like? Anything unusual about him?"

"No. Both of them were just normal, you know..." she hesitated, as if unwilling to say.

"Asian-Americans?" he finished for her.

"Yes," she said. "I'm sorry I can't be more specific."

Max shook his head. "It's okay," he said. But it wasn't.

Because what she had given him wasn't really anything at all except for something circumstantial.

Something innocent she could have been simply dramatizing. Still, a van with Yong's on the side...where had he heard that name before?

Helen was right about one thing. Alice was not the most reliable witness.

"Do you think you can find Jeffrey and the other dogs?" she asked.

"They already found Jeffrey," Helen said "He's—" her hand went to her mouth and trembled.

"Going to be okay," Max stated, trying to diffuse the situation.

"Yes," Helen said, and began to sob. "But he was hurt really bad." The two women embraced, sobbing, while Max stood by, unsure what to say or do.

Alice turned to him. "Do you think you can find who did this?"

"I do," he answered. "And thanks for your help."

"Oh," she said, wiping tears. "Anything I can do, let me know."

"I really do need to get moving," Max said.

"We understand, don't we, Helen?" Alice turned to look at her friend, who nodded.

"I'll be in touch." As he turned to go, Alice grabbed his right hand in both of hers.

"I'd love to make you dinner sometime," she cooed, recent tears now drying on her cheeks.

"Maybe," he is disentangling his hand, and moving to shake Helen's. She moved past it, and embraced him, looking into his eyes.

"Lunch was wonderful," she said.

Glancing at Alice, Max saw a look of jealousy on her face.

Great, he thought. Just what I needed. And I don't want either one of them.

46

Once he'd freed himself, Max fled to his car. In the familiar confines of the Skylark, he winced and rolled the window further down. Fortunately, it was a clear day.

The car stunk, the passenger seat smeared with dirt and what might be blood. He hoped it would not stain the aging leather.

The engine coughed to life but sputtered.

Tune up be damned. He needed to get the interior cleaned at least, after he stopped by the vet's office.

Reaching over his shoulder, he grabbed the file from his case in the back seat. Opening the app on his phone, he typed in the address.

Twenty minutes away, and it was already nearly four.

There were never enough hours in the day.

As he shifted the Buick into drive, he thought longingly of his home, only a short distance away. But he'd have to come back another time.

Looking up, he saw the two ladies standing arm in arm on the porch, waving.

Reluctantly he waved back, before leaving the curb.

HARVESTED

Chapter Six

Brake lights flashed, and Max stomped the pedal.

His heavy coupe slid to a stop. Two cars ahead was a van, and between him and it was a small import. If he hadn't braked hard, he would have crushed it like an aluminum can.

The driver hopped out, and ran forward, yelling.

There was nowhere for Max to go. Traffic in both lanes was stopped.

Shit, he thought, looking at the time on his phone.

4:35.

Max Googled the name of the vet and tapped on the number that came up.

It rang three times, then a woman answered.

"Gamble's Clinic, can I help you?"

"Yes. This is Max Boucher. I helped bring an injured dog in earlier, and I'm investigating the disappearance of the others. I'd like to stop by and ask you a few questions."

"Sure, Mr. Boucher. I'm Dr. Jerri Gamble. The staff left for the day, but I'll be around for a while."

Jerri. Max had assumed it was Jerry, but when he looked at the letterhead on the medical records again, he realized he'd misread the name.

Please God, he breathed. Let her be happily married, or ugly and not the least bit attracted to me.

He knew it to be a futile prayer. He'd stopped believing in God for good three years ago.

His priest had called on him twice at home, giving up when Max yelled at him. Jenny had believed, dragged him along to mass after mass. With her gone, he knew there was no God. If there was, he was a cruel prankster, and Max wanted nothing to do with him.

Yet he still prayed nearly every day for his wife's return. Just in case.

But a God who ignored that larger prayer would certainly ignore one as trivial as Max Boucher's desire to avoid another sexually charged encounter.

"Well, Jerri, I'm caught in traffic. I may not make it before you close."

"How close are you, Mr. Boucher?"

"It's Max. I'm at..." He strained to see the street signs at the intersection ahead.

Just then the side door of the van ahead opened, and a mid-sized oriental man stepped out. The enraged driver moved closer to him, shaking a finger.

Other drivers craned their necks to watch the action, a couple stepping from their own cars.

The driver gestured at the van's occupant. The smaller man grabbed his hand, twisted it, administered a kick, and the driver flew backward onto the hood of his car. The passenger shook his head, pointing.

The defeated driver stumbled back to his car.

The oriental man met Max's gaze. He looked familiar, and yet not.

Rolling his window all the way down while watching traffic, Max put the Skylark in park, and slid up onto the sill, still pressing the phone to his ear.

The side of the van had writing on it. He leaned out further, struggling to make out the lettering.

Yong's Takeout and Delivery.

"Mr. Boucher?" he heard in his ear as he slid back into the car.

It was just a coincidence. Had to be. How many vans could one restaurant have?

Young, but spelled wrong, Alice had said. Y-O-N-G.

There were two men inside.

The man who had put the driver of the import into his place had come out the side door.

A glance at the vehicle's side mirror told Max the driver was still in his seat and hadn't moved.

"Sorry," he said. "There was nearly an accident here."

"Why don't we skip the office? Bring your files to my place. We can have dinner."

With her husband and family, please? Max pleaded with God.

"Sounds fine," Max said. "What's your address?"

She gave him one, in Medina where some famous billionaires lived, and also the location of 13 Coins, one of his and Jenny's favorite restaurants.

Nice, he thought, and punched it into the phone. Damn, it would take him 40 minutes at best to get there.

"See you in a little under an hour," he said.

"I'll be waiting," she said, and the call ended.

That's what I'm afraid of.

***

Jerri Gamble opened the door almost as soon as he rang the bell.

A wave of relief flooded over him

She was a squat woman, maybe three inches over five feet, and in her late 50's or early 60's. Around her neck hung a stethoscope, and she was dressed in a white lab coat too long for her torso. Below that, she wore an equally long dark colored skirt and sensible shoes.

This was a long way from Queen Anne. Perhaps God did indeed answer prayers, at least the small ones.

"Mr. Boucher, I presume?" she said, looking up at him.

"Yes. Pleased to meet you Miss Gamble."

"Call me Jerri, please. Come on in. Mind the cats."

Max's gratitude faded as he entered the living room. Every potential place to sit was covered with felines of all shapes and sizes.

"Sorry about being forward and inviting you to dinner here. But as you can see, I have responsibilities. If I am away too long, the girls miss me."

Max could see the animals did, indeed, seem to follow her every move with their eyes. At least a percentage of them.

"Quite all right," he said out loud as she disappeared through a door into what he assumed was the kitchen.

"Excuse me one moment while I get them fed and get changed. Make yourself comfortable," she called.

He looked left and right. A sofa, what he thought to be his best seating option, was covered by a tabby, an orange and white monstrosity, and a white and gray feline nearly the size of a cougar. As he moved that direction, it gave him a look daring him to disturb its resting place.

The chairs were covered in similar animals, almost all over sized. On every seat, at least one, sometimes two, cats lounged, and one or more rested on the top of each chair back. The arms were occupied as well.

Max was a dog person. That didn't mean he was anti-cat, or anti-other pet.

But this many cats made him nervous. He could count at least a dozen, and he thought there were probably more.

Then he heard the familiar sound of an electric can opener.

Every cat in the room raced for the door where the vet had disappeared, and Max was left with plenty of seating choices.

He heard a chorus of meowing, followed by silence.

A few moments later, he heard a door open, and then her voice. "In here, kitties."

A second later, she appeared, propping the swinging door open.

"Come on in, Mr. Boucher. Talk to me while I cook."

Max was surprised. Out of her work clothes, Jerri was quite attractive. Her blouse was low cut, but not overly so. It accentuated her ample bosom. She still wore a skirt, but it appeared to be a different one, lighter in color, and shorter. Her feet were now clad in open toed sandals, and he saw she wore a ring on the second toe of her right foot.

She waited, watching as he looked her over, and then gestured at a seat next to a small table.

The house was older on the outside, and the living room furniture, while nice, showed its age. But the kitchen was entirely different. The appliances were modern, stainless steel, and two pans sat side by side on a gas stove.

An additional array of very nice pans hung on a rack over an oak topped island.

The living room furniture had been covered in cat hair and had the smell of a house with too many cats.

The kitchen did not smell like that at all, or even like the cat food he knew must have been there moments before.

It smelled good, and even though he'd eaten late, and not that long ago, he found himself hungry again. He pat his six-pack, hard earned at the gym, and hoped this case would not be the cause of its demise.

The presence of a jar of what looked like homemade salsa, and a stack of delightful looking tortillas promised he'd probably love dinner.

"I hope you don't mind spicy?"

"Not at all," Max said, mouth now watering. "Hotter the better."

"Good," she said. "My mother was full-blooded Mexican, and her mother lived with us for a time. My dad was a Navajo from Arizona. I don't think we ever had a dull meal, so I really don't know much about cooking anything else."

"Fantastic," he said. Lunch, real Italian. For supper, real Mexican. At least the food part of the day was good.

"So, what questions can I answer for you?" she asked.

"I'm sure you know about the dogs disappearing around Queen Anne."

"I do. It is quite odd. None of those I know about are even papered."

"I think the dognapers are avoiding those on purpose."

"For what reason?"

"They want animals who aren't as valuable. Won't be missed."

"Why are you involved? I talked to the police. I thought they were investigating."

"A friend on the force referred the owners to me. There just isn't much they can do. With budget cuts, the emphasis is on major crimes. There have been no ransom demands. Until today, there have been no threats of harm or injured animals. Just a bunch of mutts disappearing. Hell, until this afternoon there was nothing but circumstantial proof these were even thefts at all and not a series of runaways."

Beef dropped into a skillet sizzled, and the aroma of frying onions, peppers, and chilies filled his nostrils.

"I'm really looking for the one thing I am missing so far in this case. A motive. The police gave me a file, with a suspect even, but I don't get the angle."

"Was that the Chijon family angle?"

"Yeah, how did you know?"

"Listen, the guy seemed really nice. The police, even the animal activists have no proof he did anything wrong. They don't have proof he didn't either."

"Then you think he's innocent?" Something fabulous simmered behind her, and Max almost wanted to get up and look.

"I think he should be presumed innocent until he's proven guilty."

"I'm okay with that," Max stated.

Her gaze rested firmly on him, and she said nothing for a few beats, as if determining if he were telling the truth. Max returned her stare until she dropped her eyes.

"What do you want me to do, Mr. Boucher?"

"Call me Max," he said. He felt like he'd been repeating that all day long. "The police lab will take forever to get information back to me, if they will touch it at all, about dogs. I wondered if you had a lab we could work with."

"We do. They're busy as well, and not cheap. But they handle animal DNA all the time, for many different reasons."

She went back to stirring, and Max was glad. He would hate for anything to burn.

"I also thought you might be able to look over the dogs' records. Maybe you would see something I don't, a common thread that might tie them together."

"I can look, but I can't think of a single trait they all share."

"Do you ever treat any unusual dog injuries?"

"You mean like from fighting?"

"Yes."

"Not anymore. There was a big ring here in Seattle a few years ago. Moved fights around. I reported the injuries I saw, and the cops broke them up. Gambling, I think, was the primary charge, along with animal cruelty."

"Could they be reorganizing?"

Jerri laughed. "Since the Michael Vick scandal, dog fighting is much less popular. And none of these dogs were fighting breeds. In fact, every dog on your list, at least the ones I know, are almost overly friendly. And the injuries I saw today aren't consistent at all with fighting."

What are they consistent with?"

"I'd rather not say until I do further tests tomorrow, but my first guess would be surgery."

"Surgery?"

"Not a normal surgery you would expect on a dog, especially an unpapered mutt."

A plate appeared in front of him, and he stopped talking. A tortilla, still open, held a bed of chopped steak, red and green peppers, onions, and an enticing smelling sauce, but just enough to coat the meat. The pepper smell burned the inside of his nose just slightly.

A second later, Jerri set a pan on the table, filled with refried beans. The jar of salsa he'd seen came next, with a fork sticking out of the top.

"You wrap your own, or you need a hand?"

Max expertly folded the tortilla, and set the resulting burrito to the side, then dipped a large portion of beans onto his plate and placed some of the salsa on the side.

Jerri fixed her own plate and sat across from him. Picking up his heavenly filled tortilla, Max took a large bite.

Perfect.

"I'll be happy to look over the files you have when we are done eating," she said. "And I will share the results of the tests once I stabilize my patient. Probably tomorrow. Maybe we can come up with something after all."

Max mumbled an affirmative around a mouthful.

***

Other than the food, it had been a discouraging evening.

Jerri Gamble, an attractive older woman, and clearly a competent vet and animal lover, specifically cats, made clear by the dozens of felines that joined them in the living room after dinner, had in the end been no help at all. They went through all of the files without finding a single common thread or any ideas of a possible motive.

His stomach was full of delightful food, however. Max was thankful, at least tonight, that he lived alone.

He'd almost turned left, headed back toward Queen Anne, after he left Medina and got on the 520.

Only once in the last three years had he spent the night in his house in Queen Anne.

That had been early on, and he'd been drunk and passed out. He was more careful now.

Still, the temptation arose to go have a look. Just a quick one.

Things might look different tonight. He might see something vital, a clue to where Jenny had gone.

The house did look different, at various times of day. With the changing seasons.

Still, time after time he found nothing, and tonight, he thought the house was likely too close to Helen, Alice, and the case.

He turned right, giving the old Skylark some gas to keep it from dying.

Although there was a chill in the air, he rolled down the window, at least a little. First thing in the morning, the car needed to be cleaned inside.

There was too much to do.

Had he, a moment ago, been thankful he lived alone? That was just the Mexican dinner talking, his knowledge of its aftereffects. Truth be told, Max was lonely.

He missed Jenny, missed Samantha, and missed having a family.

Didn't they call that the American dream? He'd had it. Wife, kids, pets. House. Cars. Career.

Shit, the time with Miss Gamble's cats, the dogs that were part of this investigation, made him long for another pet. At least someone would greet him at the door with enthusiasm when he returned home.

But he couldn't replace Houston. No other dog would be the same. And the few times he'd even tried to date, things had ended awkwardly, and he'd gone home alone.

"You can't replace her, ever," Trudy had told him after one failed evening. "But it doesn't mean you have to stay alone."

Max knew in his heart Jenny was still out there, so being with someone else felt like cheating. No one would condemn him, he knew. But he would know and condemn himself.

And when he found Jenny again, what would he tell her? What excuse would make his actions okay?

None.

So, he remained by himself. Wife missing. No pets. But there were times he knew he could use some help.

Maybe he should call that therapist after all, the one Trudy wanted him to talk to.

***

Shorty's was open all night. The club was supposed to close at 2, but long after "last call" the bar next to his office continued to serve something at least, and the local cops, some regular patrons, looked the other way as long as things didn't get too wild.

Sometimes they would organize a raid, for one reason or another, and things would quiet for a day or two, and then the usual routine would resume.

There were worse bars in the area. Max didn't mind at all. Often he went in, even when he got home late.

Not tonight. He took the narrow set of stairs that led to the upper floor and his tiny apartment.

Max gripped his stomach, hearing it gurgle as he ascended.

Maybe he should have passed on seconds.

At the top of the stairs, he struggled with his key, his stomach now cramping.

"Come on, come on," he mumbled to himself.

The lock did not click when he turned the key, and he was instantly alert.

He never left the door unlocked.

Max set the case with the files on the floor and eased inside after drawing his pistol.

He slapped the switch on the wall and the light came on.

A figure sat on his couch.

"Hello Max," a familiar voice said.

Max slid his gun back into place.

He wished people would stop doing this to him. Didn't anyone just make an appointment anymore?

HARVESTED

Chapter Seven

"Jesus, Frank. You could have been killed," Max said

"Care to go downstairs for a drink?"

"Really, I could have just shot you."

"You were always pretty good on the range."

The man sitting on his couch wore a rumpled suit. Knowing the Seattle Police Commissioner, it had been pressed that morning, probably near perfect. But Frank Grabel rarely had short days, and rarely ended up looking as good at the end of them as he did at the beginning.

"What are you doing here, Frank? Ever hear of calling ahead?"

"Tony says you're working a case for us."

"Working a case for you? Not exactly."

"Fine, one he referred to you." The commissioner stood. "I am."

"He also tells me you are still investigating Jenny's...disappearance."

Max bristled at the way he said the last word. His hesitation.

"Listen Grabel, I'm not a cop anymore. Nothing I'm doing is illegal, and I'm a licensed P.I. Whatever your issue is, you can take it back downtown with you."

"Calm down Max. Why don't we go get that drink?"

"Because I've had a long fucking day, and I have better Scotch up here than that shit Shorty's serves," he spat angrily.

"Then we can stay here. But you need something, and so do I."

"On second thought, let's go downstairs. If we're going to talk, I'd rather be in a bar than my apartment."

"Why's that Max?"

"There will be witnesses. And Frank, give me a few minutes, and I'll meet you there."

"Is there a problem?"

"I had Mexican earlier."

Frank hurried out the door and down the stairs.

***

Shorty's wasn't just a bar.

Scantily clad women circled the room, clearly available for more personal pleasures, should one desire.

Max never desired. He met Frank outside the front door.

The bouncer at the door smiled at him when they approached, then frowned at the suit following him.

"Evening Max," he said. The bar owners and patrons liked him, because he kept his mouth shut about the extracurricular activities and could be counted on to intervene and help take out anyone who caused trouble.

"Who's your friend?" the man asked, after they shook hands. "Looks like a cop."

"He's cool. At least for tonight."

"You sure?"

"He's with me."

"Good enough. Just be sure he doesn't...disrupt things."

"I'm familiar with what goes on here," Frank said. "See no evil, and all that."

The bouncer nodded and stepped aside.

The smell always hit him first, and Max smiled. Two years ago, he would have cringed. In fact, had the first time.

Now he welcomed it. He didn't smoke himself, never had. Jenny had hated cigarette smoke, and on the frequent occasions he rode with partners who smoked, or spent time with perps that did, she made him shower and threw his clothes in the wash right away. She didn't even want the remotest hint of it in the house.

Max never knew why, but supposed it went back to her childhood. Something in her past that made her hate it.

Even when she'd disappeared and the temptation had been the greatest, he hadn't been able to start.

Frank smoked though, an occupational hazard.

And Shorty's smelled like smoke, but a blend of two kinds, one always legal, one recently legalized and even before that often ignored when bigger problems loomed in the city.

It wasn't Frank's first time at Shorty's either, and so he knew about the mix of the world's oldest profession and the most common legal addiction in the United States. An addiction he and Max shared, although Max thought himself far from an alcoholic and Frank a bit closer to one.

They found a table, one in a corner where they could see the door, and far enough away from the speakers blaring seductive music so they could hear each other.

A scantily clad waitress, Lily her name was, or so Max thought, came over and took their order.

Two Scotch rocks, doubles.

The well was Chivas, not Max's favorite, but drinkable.

"What do you want, Frank?" he finally said. "It's not like you to lower yourself to visiting my digs in the delightful community of Beacon Hill, and visit one of its finer establishments with me, without a reason."

"Perceptive as always, eh Max?"

"Once a dick, always a dick," Max joked. Then waited.

Frank drained his drink, signaled for another. "You mind?" he asked, patting his pocket.

"Nope," Max replied, lying. He seemed to be doing a lot of that the last couple of days.

Franks took a moment to light up. "I'm in a bit of a bind here."

"I see that," he replied, studying Frank as he pulled smoke deep into his lungs, and let it out his nose.

"If I share with you what I know, you'll dig even deeper into this case. Which will serve my needs, or rather the department needs, well."

"But?" Max asked.

"But it will likely put you in danger. The problem is, I can't commit the resources to this I would like to."

"Why's that?"

"Budget. Not a big enough crime. In fact, all the evidence that some kind of crime is occurring is at the moment circumstantial."

"You're the commissioner. You could operate outside the rules if you really wanted to."

"We've had this talk Max. People watch me and what I do."

"You've done it before."

"I did. And paid for it."

"But when I needed it, you didn't." Max's angst surprised him. He hadn't known he was still so angry over Frank's role in shelving Jenny's case.

"I tried Max. We've been over it. We had nothing. Two women taken. Families murdered. If you'd been home earlier, you might not be here. Whoever did...whatever happened, was a pro. Not a bit of usable evidence at either scene. No bodies found, ever. The case went cold."

"No one told you to close it."

"No, Max. I did it before they told me to, because it was coming anyway. You knew it, and so did I."

"But I didn't give up. You did."

"Stop looking for someone to blame. This is no one's fault."

Max drained his Scotch with a wince. It was going to be a long night, and he needed to calm down.

"Frank, it's just..."

"Jesus, Max! You think I don't know? You think it doesn't eat me up too? You think I don't wonder what would have happened if I left the case open a bit longer? That I don't wonder if maybe, just maybe we could have caught a break? I held out as long as I could, and you know it. Why do you think I'm here?"

"Why are you here, Frank? Why do you think I don't see Tony as much anymore? Seeing anyone from the department brings all this back up again." He slammed his fist into the table and ordered another. The mediocre liquor at Shorty's didn't come cheap, but he hoped Frank would be picking up the tab. If not, his bank account had just gotten a five-thousand-dollar boost. One he was rapidly reducing.

"I'm here to help you Max. With this case."

"Then get the fuck on with it."

"You talked to the ladies in Queen Anne. Tony told you there was more, before that. Dogs from shelters, all over the city. Even beyond, we think. Hard to be sure."

"Motive?"

"I have no idea. But it has to be something."

"Why are you so sure?"

"Simple. The Chijon family, Korean mob gone underground in the late 1990's. For a while I suspected a dog fighting ring, but it just makes no sense."

"Already looked down that road. Then what does?"

A shrug. "I'm still not sure. But I do know this. Whoever is taking dogs, let's say for argument's sake, the Chijon family, are making an investment. They have to be doing it peacefully somehow. Not even the friendliest dogs would go with a stranger willingly. I'd guess tranquilizers."

"That's a potential lead."

"Unless they are killing them right away. But besides the one today, a few have been found safe. I doubt that."

"Hold it. Other missing dogs have been found?"

"Usually they come back. Not any in Queen Anne so far. But elsewhere."

"I need names, Frank."

"You'll have them in the morning. A package will come to your door. I'm giving you everything we have; stuff Tony didn't even know about."

"Um, good. Thanks." Max studied the commissioner, not understanding his motives either.

"They have to be taking the dogs, dead or alive, somewhere."

"I understand that. Warehouse district near one of the piers?"

"Probably. Some addresses are in the file."

"So where are they getting the tranquilizers?"

"Likely a vet. They would have the easiest legal access."

"Why do you assume they have legal access?"

Frank stayed silent. He downed the rest of his drink and signaled with a single finger. One more round.

Max let him stew. The waitress arrived with new glasses for both of them, and a check.

To his relief, Frank offered a couple of crumpled twenties and a ten, and the waitress disappeared.

Max drained his other glass, then sipped from the new arrival.

"These guys are careful. Narcs can't find a thing. And two of the dogs who returned are dead."

"Dead?"

"When they came back, the owners received anonymous mail the next day. Both were sick, with cancer. The papers were test results. Both owners sought treatment, but it was too late."

"The others that returned?"

"Owners got medical records too. Nothing as serious. But every dog that came back was unhealthy, in one way or another."

"So, whoever is taking them is also making sure they're healthy?"

"That's why we suspect they aren't killing them initially."

"So only healthy dogs are being taken, but not killed. You don't think they are being used to train fighters, because they vary in size and breed, with no emphasis on more aggressive ones?"

Frank Grabel nodded.

"So essentially, with a bit more evidence than I have, you've come to the same conclusions, but you've been gathering evidence how long?"

"A year at least. But this has been going on longer than that, between the shelters and dog's disappearing."

"That's why they're taking domestics rather than strays?"

"Stray numbers are down, but we have no proof what's happening to them, or if or when they come back if they are unhealthy."

"Then what are you saying?"

"Your investigation of the disappearance of a dozen dogs in Queen Anne is the tip of the iceberg. In Seattle, over the last year, maybe longer, dozens of dogs have disappeared."

"Dozens?"

"Another reason we don't think it's a fighting ring. Not even the biggest rings need those kind of numbers."

"No one knows why, and you know almost nothing about the how?"

"You've figured out as much about that in the last couple of days than we have so far."

"Great."

"This is big Max. Be careful."

"Be careful? That's all you've got?"

"And this. If you find something solid, a real lead, something illegal we can act on, call me. Personally."

A business card hit the table. With a number handwritten on the back. "That's my cell," Frank said, sliding out of the booth.

"Thanks, I think," Max answered.

Frank waved dismissively and staggered away.

Shit, Max thought. Why did I let Tony talk me into this?

He left a ten on the table, what he thought would be an appropriate tip, and staggered out of Shorty's and up to bed.

Chapter Eight

His phone rang. Loud.

Fuck. Should have left that on silent.

How many doubles had he and Frank shared?

Too goddamn many for Max's head.

It rang again. Kept ringing.

He rolled over. Reached for the device, and the sound stopped.

Oh, that many. He covered his eyes with his hand, shading them from the light.

Light?

What time was it? Max rubbed his eyes, squinting at the screen. Nine-thirty.

Had he set up some kind of appointment?

He didn't think so.

And didn't recognize the number.

The phone rang again, and he swiped the screen to answer before recognizing his screaming need to pee.

Scrambled to his feet as he said, "Hello?"

"Mr. Boucher?"

The voice sounded familiar. "Yes?"

Max was still wearing his jeans from the night before. Struggled to undo them one handed.

"It's Dr. Gamble."

Doctor Gamble. Gamble. Oh, the vet.

"Yes!" he answered, his enthusiasm coming as much from the fact his belt and jeans were now undone, and he was crossing the threshold into his bathroom. "What can I do for you?"

"Are you okay?" she asked.

His underwear slid down.

Relief was only seconds away, but in a room with horrid acoustics.

"Hang on just a sec," he said, and muted the phone.

Splashing relief followed. Max tilted his head back, stretching as he relieved himself. God, his head ached.

Cheap Scotch, and too much of it.

"Mr. Boucher?" a distressed voice said from the phone.

He looked over.

Shit. He'd hit speaker instead of mute.

Frantic pulling up of clothing and zipping followed. As if she could see through the phone, rather than just hear.

Which meant she had just heard...

Laughter followed.

"Sorry, I meant to mute the phone."

More laughter.

Great, just great.

"Miss Gamble?"

The laughter slowed. "I'm sorry," she said.

"No," he said. "I'm sorry. I just...."

A long pause followed.

"It's okay, Max. I—good morning."

"Um, yes," he said awkwardly. "What can I do for you?"

"Max, I-um-it might be good. But it might be bad too. Can you come to the office?"

"Sure," give me..." he trailed off. Took a quick pit sniff. "Give me about an hour."

"You bet," she said. He heard more giggles as the call ended.

Wonderful start to the day, he thought, and stripped off his clothes for a shower.

***

He got in the car twenty minutes later, knowing he'd be late, but determined to stop for coffee anyway.

The ibuprofen had taken the edge off at least but hadn't removed the ache entirely.

Driving across the city prohibited him from applying the preferred hangover remedy: hair of the dog.

Turning the key, he groaned. After a sputtering start, the car died. Max pumped the accelerator, and it started again. He feathered the gas, and it stayed running.

Then the smell hit him.

Jesus. He needed to get the car cleaned too. This morning. Now it would have to wait.

He rubbed his temples and shifted into drive.

Max was a creature of habit, and though he knew he should vary his routine, do things differently and not be so predictable, he took the same route he always took, from his house toward Queen Anne. About halfway, he realized he didn't remember the address of the vet's office. Last night, or early evening, as it had turned out, he went to Dr. Gamble's house instead.

At the next stoplight he reached for his phone, and tapped the navigation app. The address was still entered from the night before. He'd already driven past the turn, so would have to circle back.

Glancing in the mirror, he noticed a dark colored van a couple cars behind. He kept an eye on it as he changed lanes. It changed lanes right after he did.

He moved into the left turn lane, planning to go around the block.

The van followed.

No big deal, except the driver hung back. Didn't take the open right lane like Max expected him to.

At the next intersection, Max took another left. Checked his mirror. The van was still there.

Even odder.

"At the next intersection, take a left. Then your destination will be on the right." The mechanical feminine voice on his phone told him.

"Fuck you," he mumbled, paying too much attention to the mirror now, but suspicious.

His instinct told him the van was following him, but why?

Passing up the next turn, he went two more blocks.

Jesus, Max. Taking the route around Cock Robbins barn. His grandfather's expression for the long way.

Took a left. This felt like NASCAR.

The van took it, too.

Took the next left, and it was still following.

"Your destination is on the left," the voice said.

Max took a right into a parking area, squealed into a space, and slammed the car into park.

There was no need to shut it off, it died on its own.

But he took out the keys and stood quickly, running out to the street.

The van was stopped at the corner. The driver looked back at him. Saluted, and pulled back into traffic.

Max realized he'd been a horrid witness. Dark van, no plate numbers.

What an idiot.

It was time to be more careful.

He walked to the corner, and used the crosswalk, looking down at his phone.

Twenty minutes late. Not bad for a hangover morning and shaking a tail.

But he hadn't stopped for coffee. He hoped Dr. Jerri Gamble made as good a brew as she did food.

***

The bell rang as he walked through the door, something Max always found irritating. He didn't always like people to know he was coming, even when the purpose of his visit was friendly or he was invited, like now. Most businesses had them, and he understood the purpose. But as with many things, his understanding did not diminish aggravation.

A cheery 'Hello" came from a room somewhere in the back. No one sat at the reception desk.

"Max is that you?" followed his silent failure to answer.

"Yes," he answered.

"Come on back." Her voice was cheery but concerned.

When he entered the back room, he saw Jeffrey laying there. The dog's tail thumped against the exam table.

"Did you figure out what happened to him?" Max gestures to the bandage.

"Yes and no."

"What does that mean?"

"Look at this," she said, tossing a file onto the table next to him.

It landed upright, and he saw the words "kidney disease probable" highlighted.

"Kidney disease? In a dog?"

"Yes. It's quite common in some breeds, but usually doesn't occur until dogs are older, or at least it goes undetected until they start showing symptoms."

"Wouldn't you catch it on, like, an annual physical or something?"

"It's not like with people. We don't draw blood every time a dog comes in, and people are way laxer with their pet's annual physicals than their own. Which is saying something. When was the last time you had a physical with a full blood work-up?"

Max didn't want to answer. The department required annual physical and psychological evaluations for all Senior Detectives. He'd just about been due for his when he left, so he could reasonably say four years.

And he never took Houston as often as he should either. Houston was healthy, a good dog.

"What does that have to do with this?"

"Jeffery is fine, except for a small incision that bled a lot. He probably tore it open after he was dropped in the park. It looks like he was headed for surgery."

"Surgery?"

"For a kidney transplant."

"In a dog?"

"Oh yes. They are actually quite common in cats, but dog programs are rare."

"Why?"

"Well, dog transplants are not as successful. And there are not as many dog research programs, so owners have to find their own donors."

"I don't understand."

"Look, Max, the process is complicated. And until recently, there was a program at the University of California. It got put on hold due to lack of funding. More recently a private one cropped up."

"Private?"

"Not a university. The source of the funds is an anonymous philanthropist."

"And?"

"Just eight weeks ago, this article." She tossed a magazine on top of the chart. "Mutts as Universal Donors," the title of the article read.

He scanned the first few paragraphs, the light dawning.

"It used to be donors were selected from the same breed of dog, preferably young dogs, right? But this says mutts can be matched to several breeds."

"Exactly."

"Then Jeffrey here, and the other dogs were taken because they are mutts?"

"Right again."

"What we have is motive."

"A possible motive. And this is why Jeffrey was returned." She tapped the chart. "He isn't a candidate. He has the early stages of kidney disease."

"And why don't they return the other dogs?"

"Well, with cats, usually the recipient's owner must adopt the donor. There must be something similar going on here. Whoever is doing this could not return the donor dog. The owner would notice the incision, and the dog often requires special care for a while."

"So, the only dogs returned are those with health issues that prohibit donation, and the other dogs are probably still alive."

"Probably. Providing the surgeries went well."

"The mutts are essentially an organ farm?"

"Yes."

"But dozens have disappeared just here in Seattle."

"They must be supplying a nationwide demand from here."

"I just can't believe there would be that many owners looking for this."

"You'd be surprised Max. Dogs are like kids to many people. You know that."

He did. And understood all too well. "What they are doing is not really illegal, other than stealing dogs."

"Not strictly speaking. It's unethical, and maybe illegal if they are doing the work in an unlicensed clinic."

"What would they get for that?"

"A fine, and a scolding to stop practicing."

"Shit."

"I don't know what to say, Max. I almost admire them for what they are doing."

"What about the owners they are taking pets from?"

"I guess they figure they will get another dog. A mutt is a mutt."

Just then the bell over the door rang.

"That must be Susan, coming to get Jeffrey."

"I'm going to run to the restroom. I'll be right back," Max said.

The vet covered her mouth, and he heard her giggle. "Down the hall, last door on the right. No need to call anyone while you're in there," she said.

Max groaned and blushed, fleeing as quickly as possible.

***

Outside the door, he heard excited voices in the hallway.

He double checked his zipper. He'd had enough bathroom embarrassment for one day.

Almost as soon as he rounded the corner, a familiar looking dog darted around his feet, nearly tripping him.

It looked like Helen's dog. The original missing pup, and reason for the case.

Helen appeared next.

"Come back here girl!" she called.

The pup obeyed, with one final jump. Jerri followed. She smiled at him, and he smiled back.

Max saw Helen glance at both of them, a puzzled expression on her face.

"So, what happened here?" he asked, gesturing to the dog.

"She showed up late last night, barking outside my door. I got up and let her in, and it's like she was never gone."

"Was there anything else?" he asked her, unwilling to voice his concern.

"No. Should there be?"

"You might get a package today. In the mail or on your doorstep. If you do, don't open it. Bring it to me or Jerri here first, okay?"

Helen stared at him, an almost fearful look in her eyes. Not like she was afraid of what might happen, but like a kid caught with their hand in the cookie jar. "What do you know?"

"I can't say right now. But I have a lead, a small one. I'd rather follow up on it before I answer. Just promise you'll follow my instructions exactly."

"Dr. Gamble checked her out. She seems none the worse for the experience."

"Good, good," said Max, exchanging a glance with the vet.

She didn't say anything, simply nodded an affirmative. "There's nothing obviously wrong with her. She hasn't been abused, and in fact seems to have eaten just fine. The only thing she seems starved for is affection."

"I can take care of that," Helen said. "Thank you, Max.," Helen approached and hugged him. Max felt like she used a little too much body, maybe squeezed a little too hard. But he just returned the hug and patted her back.

"You are still on the case, right?" she said when she was done.

"Of course." He tried to smile.

"I'll see you around then?" she asked.

"Please, let me know if you get anything delivered to your home today. In fact, call both of us before you open it."

Why would I need to call Dr. Gamble?"

"Just trust me."

"Okay. I'm going to get this gal home and spoil her to death."

"Great," Max said with a faked smile. "I'll be in touch."

The vet looked at him as she left. "I took my own samples. You think she'll get a package?"

"Or another kind of message. Someone wants me off this case." Something else nagged at him too. Jennifer's return felt different then Jeffrey's. It felt—staged.

"Well, if Helen gets something, if she calls me first, I will let you know. I'll call you when I get the results of the blood test."

"Thanks," Max said, and left. He walked down to the crosswalk, and back to his car.

As he opened the driver's door, the smell hit him, hard. He really needed to get it cleaned, right now.

He had nowhere else to go, so he headed for a car wash he frequented, near his old house.

He had a feeling either way things went down, his next stop that afternoon would be somewhere in Queen Anne.

Chapter Nine

"Hey Eddie."

"Hey Max."

"Can you clean up the interior for me?"

The attendant, one he knew well, opened the driver's door.

"Jesus, Max. What happened in here?"

"Do you really want to know?"

"Smells like a dog died."

"Close."

"You want me to wash the outside too?"

"Might as well do what you can."

"I'd ask about wax, but you still haven't had her painted."

"I keep meaning to, Eddie."

"I've been hearing that for five years. Damn shame. This is a fine automobile. Deserving of better than the likes of you."

"Enough preaching. Just do your best. How long do I have?"

"About an hour, maybe more," the attendant said. "This is gonna cost you extra."

"No worries," Max said, thinking of the original five grand in the bank dwindling rapidly. At least he hadn't paid for drinks the night before. Or he didn't think he had.

"Fran's still have a great Rueben?"

"You bet," Eddie replied. "You definitely have time for one of those."

Max handed over his keys. "See you in an hour or so."

As he walked away, he heard the motor catch, and sputter, then die. He heard it turn over for a full ten seconds and catch again as Eddie revved it up. He knew he'd hear about his delay of a tune up when he returned.

He smiled, remembering when Jenny had introduced him to this place, where she had her car cleaned all the time.

The car that still sat in the garage at his old house.

There likely wasn't any evidence in it. The crime hadn't happened anywhere near the garage. And nothing had happened in her car, it had been parked in the driveway.

But Max still couldn't bring himself to sell it or drive it. He'd only moved it inside and left it. The keys still hung on the hook inside the doorway, where they always had.

Thinking of his shrinking bank balance, and the bills coming due, maybe he should look into it again.

He walked into Fran's, a tiny deli on the corner, pleased to see his usual waitress still worked there.

He didn't stop to eat often when he was out this way, but when he did, he always stopped here. It had been at least six months.

"Max!" she shrieked. Nancy ran around the counter to give him a hug.

"Hey there," he said, pulling back from her.

"You ready for a real woman yet?" she asked. It was something she'd asked him often, even before Jenny was gone.

Max tried not to let it get to him. "Not yet. Not sure I can handle you."

As she ended the embrace, she pinched his ass. "By the time you're ready, your heart will be too weak to handle the likes of me."

"You're probably right. You better be looking for a stronger man."

Not for the first time, Max wondered if she was joking, or what she would do if he took her up on her offer. How far would she let it go?

All these women around him the last few days were messing with his head. He missed Jenny, every day, but there were times when he was just like any other man. He had...wants.

He didn't want to think about it. It felt like cheating.

"The usual, Max?" she asked.

"You bet. And some of that shitty coffee you serve, as long as you haven't improved it at all."

"Coming up," she said, winking.

Per his usual habit, Max sat where he could see the street and the door. He could observe anyone who approached the restaurant, and he'd be the first to see them enter.

He felt like he was being paranoid again, or still. But he had good reason.

Nancy delivered the coffee, and today's *Intelligencer*. Taking a sip of the hot liquid, he grimaced at the bitter taste, then opened the paper to the front page. Nothing new. Nothing of interest.

Flipped to the second section. Sports. New trades and new scandals populated the headlines.

Nothing unusual.

Then he flipped back to the classifieds. On a whim, he scanned the pet section.

The first part was pets for sale. It was short and contained only ads from breeders or for papered animals. The internet had pretty much killed the printed classifieds, except for a few specialties.

But as his eyes wandered down the page, he saw something unusual. The lost and found column seemed longer than normal. Some of the ads had pictures, others just descriptions.

He scanned the first several. Most were mutts. Last seen in this park, or that one. He recognized all the place names.

Some had leash laws, others were more lax locations. There were a few listings from Queen Anne, some of them dogs on his list.

The found section was really small.

His Rueben came, piled high with corned beef and onions. Nancy set his favorite mustard next to his plate.

She placed a basket, piled high with fries, next to it, with a bottle of fry sauce, something he'd discovered on a visit to a diner in Idaho, and passed on to Fran, the owner and head chef.

Not everyone liked it, but they served it to Max automatically every time he ate here.

"You look like you saw a ghost," Nancy said. "Something wrong in the paper?"

"Not at all." Max was tired of lying, but he did anyway.

He dug into the sandwich, trying to forget the odd number of ads, but without success.

***

Max walked into the parking lot of the car wash, and saw the Skylark off to the side, with the hood up.

Someone wearing blue coveralls with a red rag sticking out of his back pocket had his head buried deep in the engine compartment.

He heard swearing in Spanish as he approached.

"What's going on?" he asked.

Startled, the man rose suddenly, hitting his head on the underside of the hood.

"*Madre de Dios*!" he cursed.

Eddie came trotting over from the exit.

"Max!" he called.

"What the hell is going on with my car, Eddie?"

"You needed a tune up, *mio*," he said. "She was running horrible. This is my cousin, Jesse."

Indeed, the mechanic's name was Jesse as Max read in the circle over his pocket. The man stepped back, rubbing the back of his head.

"Your carburetor, she was all out of whack. And you needed new plugs and wires. Get in and fire her up." Jesse spun an odd-looking wrench around his finger and smiled.

"Pleased to meet you too," Max mumbled. He moved to the driver's door and found the keys in the ignition. At least the interior smelled better.

He turned the key, and the Buick started on the first crank. The idle was a little rough, and Jesse tsk-tsked, murmured something in Spanish, and ducked back under the hood. Max felt the idle change and smooth out.

"That should do it," the mechanic said, and shut the hood. Eddie handed him some money, they shook hands and embraced, and he trotted off toward the car wash.

Then Eddie came to Max's window.

"That'll be two hundred seventy-eight bucks."

"For an interior clean? No wax?"

"And a superior tune up by my cousin, Jesse."

"Which I did not ask for."

"But you needed. Face it Max, when would you have gotten around to doing it yourself?"

Eddie was right, of course. He wouldn't have. It might have gone months, until the car was nearly undrivable, before he would have made it a priority. And he had needed it.

"Thanks, Eddie."

"*Sus es mi hermano*, Max," Eddie said. "How have you been?"

"Fine, Eddie, just fine."

"You still have the house, I see," he said.

Why was everyone always so concerned with his house and when he was going to sell it? Wasn't anything his own business?

"I do Eddie."

"Are you going to sell it ever?"

"I really don't know," Max answered. "Can you take a card? I didn't grab any cash this morning," he tried to change the subject.

"Sure, Maxo. Sure," Eddie answered. "Any word on the case?"

At first Max was confused. How could Eddie know about the case with the dogs?

But of course, that wasn't the case he was referring to.

He meant Jenny.

"Nothing, Eddie. She's still missing."

"Lo siento, mi amigo."

"*Todo esta bien*," Max said, clapping him on the shoulder. He could feel the grief in the back of his mind, like a tumor, waiting for the surgeon's knife to remove it. But there was no surgery for this ailment.

There was only one way to exercise the grief. Find Jenny, one way or the other.

He and his wife had a connection, beyond a normal human one. If she was dead, he would know.

He was almost positive he would be able to sense her absence from this world.

It wasn't something he wanted to discuss with a car wash attendant, right here or now. Even if he had made sure his car was fixed too.

Max offered him the card, and Eddie swiped it. Max almost held his breath, even though he knew it would go through. There was plenty of money in that account, at least at the moment.

As he finished the transaction, asking Eddie about his wife and kids, willing to use almost anything to distract the man from asking any more about Jenny and the past, his cell phone rang in his pocket.

When he pulled it out, he saw the number.

Helen.

"He—"

"I have a package," she said before he could speak. "It says to open immediately. Should I still wait for you?"

"Yes. I'll be there in five," he told her.

Might as well see what the Buick could do now that it was running better. Things were moving much too fast around him.

***

The tires squealed as he rounded the corner. He hoped Helen had followed his instructions and called Jerri too. He might need her expertise.

As he pulled up, he saw Helen in the doorway.

"Hurry, Max," she said. "Something's wrong with Jennifer."

"What is it?"

"Don't know. She started whimpering and acting funny about an hour ago."

"An hour ago?"

"Yeah, right before the package arrived. What's going on Max?"

"The package?" he asked as he sprinted through the door. The dog, Jennifer, lay on the living room floor on her side. Her breathing was shallow, her eyes darted back and forth. Max could tell she was in pain.

A large, overstuffed manila envelope lay on the coffee table. There was no address. No postage.

"Where did this come from?" he asked.

"I heard a knock. This was on the steps."

Max ripped open the package, hoping it was not booby trapped in some way. It wasn't.

Inside was a towel, wrapped around something. He shook it out, and two syringes fell to the floor, along with a piece of paper.

On it was a typewritten list.

"I hope you opened this in time," it read. "Otherwise, the rest of this note doesn't matter."

The dog whimpered just then, and Max looked over at her. Please God, let me be in time.

"I hope you have the vet with you, Max," it said.

"Helen!" he yelled. She was right behind him.

"What?" she said. He could hear the panic in her voice.

"Get Dr. Gamble on the phone, now."

She went away, he assumed to either retrieve her cell, or her house phone, if she even had one.

The syringes were two different colors. Green and blue.

"The dog has been injected with a time sensitive capsule," the note said. "It has ruptured by now, and the animal is showing symptoms."

"No shit," he mumbled. "Come on, tell me something I don't know."

"The green syringe should be administered to the brisket, just behind the right foreleg. The blue injected in the area near the popliteal lymph node."

"What the hell does that mean?" he asked himself. Just then Helen came back.

"You have her on the line?" he asked, looking at the phone.

Her pale face nodded.

"Put her on speaker."

Helen obeyed.

"Dr. Gamble, can you hear me?"

"Yes," she said. "What's going on, Max?"

"Helen's dog. Jennifer. She's in distress, shallow breathing, probably in pain."

"Okay?" she said. "Bring her in."

"I don't think we have that kind of time," he said. "I also have the package here. In it were two syringes with instructions. I need you to talk me through them."

"Read them to me."

"The green syringe should be injected into the brisket, just behind the right foreleg."

"No problem. Move to the dog's right side."

"She is lying on her left. Now what?"

"Find the pulse behind her right foreleg and inject the syringe there."

Max kneeled over the dog. He remembered his combat training in the Marines, and how to start an emergency IV. He hoped injecting a dog was similar.

He hesitated, and Helen grabbed the syringe.

"I'll do it," she said, uncapping the needle and injecting the contents.

Jennifer whined.

Her breath came faster.

Shit, Max thought.

"She's breathing even faster."

"Read me the rest."

"Blue syringe, popliteal lymph node."

"Roll her over and inject her just forward of her left hind leg."

He rolled her over, and even before he could explain, Helen felt down the leg, and made the injection like she'd been doing it her whole life.

Jennifer's breathing slowed, almost normalized.

"Thank God," he said. "Where did you learn to do that?"

Helen knelt next to her dog, petting her, and mumbled something.

"What?" he asked.

"I was once a nurse," she said, louder.

"Is she better?" he heard from the phone. He'd forgotten the vet was still on the line.

"She seems to be," he answered.

"I hope so," Dr. Gamble said. "Get her and those empty syringes to me as fast as you can."

"Will do," he said. He looked at the dog.

One hundred pounds of mutt love. He needed to get her into his Buick and wasn't sure he could manage by himself.

"Helen, can you help me?" he asked.

Helen stared straight ahead, glassy eyed. His instincts were screaming despite the adrenaline flowing through him. Something was wrong here, and not just with the dog.

Jennifer licked her lips, even wagged her tail a little, but made no move to get up.

"I'm gonna carry you girl," he said.

Squatting, he wrapped his arms around her thick body, and managed to pick her up.

She smelled like Houston always had after a run, or a heavy fetching session. Like sweaty dog.

Suddenly, he missed his dog terribly, the faithful friend who'd been taken from him. Every time he turned around today, he was being assaulted with grief. But there was no time to dwell on his feelings.

"I got you girl," he said. He managed, just barely, to get her out the door and down the walk.

Then he got to the Skylark and realized there was no way he could get the passenger door open with her in his arms.

"Helen!" he called.

No response.

The dog was getting heavy, and Max considered himself to be in pretty good shape. He'd have to set her down.

He was about to do so, when Helen appeared at his side. She didn't say a word, but pulled the door open, and slid the seat back as far as it would go.

He was thankful she'd thought of that.

He set the dog on the seat as gently as possible.

"You'll have to squeeze in back behind me," he told her.

"Fine," she said. He opened the driver's door, and she leaned the seat forward, ducking behind it into the tiny seat in the back of the coupe.

Max climbed in after her and started the motor.

As soon as he pulled away from the curb Jennifer coughed, and her mouth yawned wide.

Before he could do anything about it, she threw up on the floor.

The smell was horrendous, and Max rolled the window down as quickly as he could.

The fresh air was chilly but smelled good.

He squealed around the corner, headed for the vet's office, pleased at how well his car was running.

At the same time, he wondered what Eddie would charge him to clean the interior for the second time in one day.

Jennifer looked at him, appearing to apologize with her eyes.

"It's okay," he said, reaching over to pat her head.

He hadn't been able to save his own dog, so long ago. Or his own Jennifer. But today, he helped save this one.

At least he hoped so.

A van slowed in front of him, and Max swerved around it, pushing the pedal to the floor.

HARVESTED

Part Two: Lost

"Anyway, it doesn't matter how much, how often, or how closely you keep an eye on things because you can't control them. Sometimes things and people just go. Just like that."

— Cecelia Ahern

HARVESTED

Chapter Ten

The bell dinged, and Max growled at it.

He was hoping Dr. Gamble would greet him with something wheeled to set the large animal on, who, now apparently feeling better, struggled in his arms as if she wanted to get down.

But instead, Jerri gestured him to carry the dog to a back room where she waited. His shoulders ached, and he struggled through the doorway.

Helen followed close behind.

"You have the syringes?" she asked.

"In the car," he said. "I didn't want to put the needles in my pocket."

"I grabbed them." Helen said. "They're right here."

She handed them over, and Jerri threw them onto the counter with a grunt.

She then began to examine the dog.

"I'll be back" Max said, headed to the restroom. There were sinks where he could have scrubbed up in the exam room, but he wanted a moment alone.

While scrubbing his hands, he looked in the mirror. Saw red rimmed steel gray eyes, a short haircut in need of a trim wildly askew, sporting two days growth of beard.

"Looking rough, Maxie boy," he whispered.

Apparently, the ladies didn't mind, but he wished they did.

Maybe Eddie and Tony were right. Maybe he should let go, at least a little. Maybe he should start to move on.

He could start by getting a dog. They couldn't be that hard to come by, and heaven knew his landlord would not object. Not as long as his checks kept clearing the bank the first of every month.

He'd have to bring it along all the time, since he was away from home so much.

Still, would that be so bad?

He thought of Houston. How he'd died defending his family. Thought about the way Jennifer had smelled when he picked her up.

Remembered the smell of blood when they'd found Jeffery yesterday. The same smell as three years ago.

He wasn't ready.

Maybe almost, he thought. He promised himself he'd keep it in mind.

After splashing water on his face, and running his wet fingers through his long hair, he left and re-entered the exam room. Jennifer wagged her tail.

"I think you have a new friend for life," Helen said, moving to hug him. She left her arms around him a bit too long for his comfort. "And Jennifer likes you too."

"So, she will be okay?" he asked.

"Seems like it. Although it will take a more thorough examination to be sure, it appears she was given some kind of poison, though I am not sure how it was timed the way it was, and just in time, an envelope was delivered containing a two-part antidote. Simple, elegant, and just scary enough."

"So why the specific points for the injection?"

"There doesn't appear to be a reason. You probably could have injected that antidote anywhere."

"Why follow those instructions then?"

"I didn't know what we were dealing with at the time."

"Do you now?"

"No. I can send the syringes to a lab. The antidote should tell us something about the poison."

"Any guesses?"

"Not yet. It really doesn't make sense at all."

"Thanks for all of your help doc. Can you make sure Helen here gets a ride home?"

"Where are you off to so fast?" she asked.

Yeah, where?" Helen chimed in.

"I have to go get my car cleaned. Again," he said, leaving before they could object.

The bell dinged as he went out too, and he swore under his breath.

One more time, and he'd break that thing off.

He headed to Eddie's place. He wanted to get there before he left for the day. He always gave Max a discount.

The engine gave a healthy roar as he pushed the accelerator to the floor.

Max smiled, for the first time in a couple of days.

***

Max turned into the parking lot still wearing the grin he'd pasted on leaving the vets.

Sure, the case was getting a little odd, a little rough.

But his car was running great, even though it stunk again.

Truth be told, it felt good to have a case that held his interest.

Whenever he was working the typical case a private dick caught, the inevitable my husband is cheating, my wife is stepping out, or we think our teen is doing drugs, he was bored, and his mind wandered. For the last three years, it only had one place to go: *Where's Jenny?*

The worst case so far, not that he'd racked up hundreds, was a set of parents. Their daughter, eighteen, had run off. The cops wouldn't take it too seriously, as it was too likely she was just sowing her wild oats.

The cops were right.

Max had found her. In a porn studio, giving as good as she got. She offered him a freebie not to take her back.

He declined, and then had to face actually telling them. He did, with shaking voice and hands.

The whole time he'd been thinking of his Samantha, and how much he would give to have her back. He watched the girl's father swing from calling Max a liar, to looking at the pictures he provided and sobbing, to threatening to call the law on what was a dirty, but legal business.

Max didn't have the heart to tell him his daughter was clearly using. The cops could arrest her, sure, but they would not bring her back to her parents. They would send her to jail first, probably a short sentence for her first offense if she had not been arrested before. Then she might turn to worse occupations using her body, if there was such a thing. Then would come prison and if reform never came, death.

Max had simply nodded, sympathized, and collected his check.

He then went back down to the porn studio and waited.

When she came out, he gave her a business card for a friend who was a counselor, ran a clinic for girls just like her, and a church called XXX Ministries.

He had no idea if it would work for her, if she would even call, or just throw it away.

But he'd tried.

This case was different. Max was a dog lover and felt like he could make a difference. The case held more intrigue than peeking in windows. The results would not be divorce papers filed, or a dirty little secret hidden from a spouse who wasn't cheating after all.

The case held sinister elements too, and he worried about those, but not overly much.

He knew he was a good detective. He'd figure it out. Hopefully before anyone else got seriously hurt.

"Eddie here?" he rolled down the window as the attendant ran out to his car.

"No, sir," the kid said. "He left a bit ago. Family emergency, he said."

"Humph," Max said. "Well, I need my car cleaned again."
"This the one Jesse worked on?"

"Yes."

"Was there a problem?"

"Nope, another incident, unfortunately."

The attendant leaned in to take a look, and the smell hit him. "Shit!"

"Puke, actually," Max said.

"Okay. We're not too busy. I'll get you in right away."

"Eddie usually gives me a discount," Max tried.

"For shit and puke? Sorry. Not the second time in one day."

"The first time was blood."

"What?" the attendant replied.

"Never mind," Max said. "I'm gonna run to Fran's for a shake. I'll be back."

"See you soon," the man said. Max slid out of the driver's seat, and the attendant wrinkled his nose as he pulled the car toward an open bay, equipped with a carpet shampooer, vacuums, and various air fresheners.

***

Nancy was both surprised and pleased to see him again.

Fran's milkshakes were legendary, and he ordered a mint-chocolate chip, whip and cherry.

Nancy commented about the whip, he ignored her with a smirk.

He sat in his usual booth, so he could see the door.

A few sips in, he saw Eddie running toward the diner.

He burst inside.

"Eddie!" Nancy, the waitress, greeted.

Eddie glanced at her but said nothing. His face was red, his features twisted with rage.

He came straight for Max, not varying his route at all. Max moved to stand.

A much larger man than Eddie, he typically would tower over him.

But the smaller man hit him in the chest, and Max sat back down, hard, not because the blow had been enough to topple him, but from shock.

"*Que es esto?*" Eddie screamed. "*Que es esto? Donde esta mi perro?*"

"What?" Max said. The words came too fast for his weak Spanish.

"*Donde esta mi perro?* Where is my dog?"

"Your dog?" Max said. "Calm down, Eddie. How would I know where your dog is?"

"You show up this morning, something about dog blood and some *hermosa* you dig, *verdad?*"

"Yeah, yeah. All true Eddie."

"I get a call from my wife. My dog went missing when she was out walking him. He took off for a few seconds, running after God knows what, and didn't come back. She chased him, and he was gone."

"Eddie, calm down."

"No, Maxo. No. I call the shop to tell them what's going on, they tell me you are back to have your car cleaned again. Dog puke this time."

"I can explain Eddie."

"Makes me think maybe Max isn't who he seems. Maybe you know more than you say."

"Eddie—"

"Where's my dog Max? Where's my fucking dog?"

"I don't know, Eddie, but if you give me a minute—"

"You are private eye, yes?"

"Yes."

"You are looking into something with dogs, yes?"

"Yes. What makes you think your dog disappearing has anything to do with that?"

"My wife—she go looking for my dog. She no find him. But look. *Madre de Dios,* look!"

Eddie held out a brown piece of paper. "This is why I call the shop. To see what is going on. This is why I come find you."

Max took the paper. On it, in careful handwriting, were the words, "Max Boucher is off his leash. Ask him about your dog."

"You see? You see?" Eddie exclaimed.

Max looked again. He looked up at his friend.

Eddie's head was in his hands, face covered.

"Eddie, what kind of dog do you have?"

"A mutt. Nothing special, except Maria—*mi espousa*—loves that dog. Sometimes I think more than she loves me."

"I'll find him."

"You're the reason he was taken."

"That might be true. What's his name?"

"Jesus," Eddie replied.

"You have a picture?"

Eddie took one from his pocket. It was crumpled.

Another medium sized mutt. Back, with some brown patches, socks on two of four paws.

Nothing special, except to Eddie and his family.

"I'll get to the bottom of this," Max said.

"Please," Eddie replied.

"Let's go." Max dropped a five on the table for a tip, looking longingly at the hardly touched shake he was leaving behind.

He followed Eddie out the front door and back towards the car wash.

Nancy looked at him in puzzlement as they left. His good mood from earlier had evaporated.

HARVESTED

Chapter Eleven

His car sat out front, again. The places where paint was still present sparkled in the early evening light.

The dull primer remained, well, dull.

The weatherman promised that tomorrow the sun would go away, and they'd be back to the typical Seattle haze.

Max looked forward to it. His mood was dark again.

The whole thing pissed him off.

Someone wanted him to stop looking into the disappearance of the dogs.

They'd tried to warn him off, twice now.

He could call the police at this point. Tony, or the commissioner. Hell, he had a case now.

The threats to him were vague, but real.

Clearly the last couple disappearances were not mutts running off. Dr. Gamble had as much as proven that.

But it was about more than dogs missing, more than the money, and the ladies who had hired him.

Max knew what it was like to lose a pet. Maybe the pain had been dulled in light of the other pain surrounding him at the time, but it had been just as real.

And whoever was taking these animals was making it personal.

Not that Max had a lot of friends. Not as of three years ago. But those he did have he cared about.

Eddie was one, distant, but always there.

No way could whoever was doing this know about their relationship. Regardless, they were trying to use what they did know.

That made him angry.

The best lead he had was the suspected contact in the Chijon family. And this Yong's restaurant. He'd hoped to find a more solid connection before confronting them.

Fuck that.

He grabbed his phone as he slid into the driver's seat of the Buick.

It fired up on the first try. Stayed running, no hesitation. He revved the motor.

Eddie gestured to him, and he rolled the window down.

"What are you going to do, Max?"

"Find your dog, Eddie. Find the rest."

"You be careful," he said. "These are bad men, Max. I feel *en mi corazon.*"

"Thanks Eddie. I will," he said. Rolled up the window, and realized he had no idea where he was going. Grabbed his phone.

Battery 14%, the screen read.

He'd have to hope it was enough.

Tapped the mic in the corner. "Navigate to Yong's Restaurant," he commanded.

"Which one would you like?" came the answer.

He looked at the screen and tapped the closest one.

12 minutes ETA, according to the GPS.

Good.

He tossed the phone onto the seat, leaving the navigation on, even though he was comfortable with the directions.

Max knew this city like the back of his hand.

Revved the motor again and slammed the car into drive. Squealed the tires as he pulled onto the street.

In his mirror, he saw a familiar dark van pull out behind him.

Fuck them. Let them follow.

Still, might as well make it fun.

He pushed the pedal to the floor and weaved around the car in front of him.

***

Max would have been much faster than the van on a straightaway. Unfortunately, there weren't any on the way to his destination.

Clearly, they were done hiding the fact they were following him.

He was done hiding the fact he knew it.

Max made no attempt to disguise his route. It might mean whoever was at the restaurant, if anyone, would know he was coming.

He had no problem with that at all.

A part of him said this was a bad idea. He had a .45 with two clips, and a .38 in his ankle holster.

Eighteen shots of .45, and six of .38 should be enough to handle any trouble.

But he wasn't a cop anymore. Not that even then, he could've rushed in, guns blazing. Besides, more than likely that wouldn't help with the case, and there were civilians to be considered. I mean people might actually eat at this place. As busy as the truck seemed to be and the fact they had three locations had to mean something.

Hell, he might have eaten take out from there. He and Jenny frequently ate from the little white boxes with red lettering, and after Samantha came along, it became a frequent treat. His daughter loved it, learned to use chopsticks, and had been pretty good with them.

And her daddy often returned from his job late, or at least at odd hours.

Every turn, every time he turned around, Max was reminded of what he had taken for granted and lost. At the moment, it just made him angrier.

"You have arrived," the mechanical voice said from the passenger seat.

"Showtime," he said. But adding to his frustration was the fact there were no parking spaces in front of the restaurant. Or in the parking lot on the corner, at a quick glance.

Shit. He circled the block. Still, nothing.

Christ on a crutch.

He felt like double parking and just running inside.

That would be stupid.

This whole thing is stupid.

Maybe. But this morning he'd saved Jennifer. In his mind, saved a Jenny, when he couldn't save his own. Now Eddie was in need, his dog Jesus a fresh take.

He could save Jesus now. Pronounce it Jeezus rather than Hay-sous.

Somehow soothe his soul, at least that's what it felt like.

Max circled another block, farther away this time. Nothing. One block more.

He glanced in the mirror. The van was gone.

No matter. They must know where he was going and were probably waiting for him.

Soon, he would know who *they* were.

A space opened up, in a pay lot.

Max pulled in, went to the pay station, and paid for six hours with his debit card, although he had no intention of taking that long.

But better safe than sorry. It was hard to pursue a lead on foot, even tougher using public transportation.

The sun had already sunk below the surface of the sound, and the streets in this section of town were well lit.

He checked the .45, in a shoulder holster. Secure. Checked the .38.

Busy streets.

Careful, Max. The voice in his head was a combination of his own and Eddie's.

He knew he was walking into danger.

Maybe.

Or walking in to order dinner and scope the place out.

The crowd thinned as he approached the restaurant. Half a block away, he saw there were now two parking spaces open right in front of the door, and a neon sign in the window read "Closed."

It had read "Open" when passed by not long ago. He'd checked.

The parking spaces had all been full. He stepped into a doorway across the street and watched.

A couple came out of the door. The man seemed angry, and the woman was crying.

"You can't close in the middle of dinner!" he yelled.

"Oh yes, we can," a voice answered. "You get out now. You no come back."

The couple got into a lower-end C-class Mercedes and squealed away from the curb into traffic.

A moment later the outside light went off.

The one in the dining room, in the window behind the "Closed" sign, followed.

The red neon was the only illumination still coming from the place.

From his pocket, his phone chirped.

A message?

Keeping to the shadows, he took it out to look.

"Low Battery. 4%. Consider plugging in your phone," the screen said.

Max pressed and held the power button, until the screen cycled, and the phone shut off.

He checked his holster once again, making sure his weapon was ready.

Putting his hands in his pockcts and keeping his head down to hide his face from the streetlights overhead, he kept to the shadows, and approached Yong's Korean Food.

***

There were a number of ways to approach a building, and a situation like this. Stealth was one, but it was too late for that.

Clearly the occupants of the restaurant knew he was coming.

Maybe. It looked like they'd closed up to prepare.

He could storm the place and felt like doing that. But he was alone. And they would be waiting.

He could approach boldly, but with a bluff.

They didn't have to know he was alone or didn't have some kind of back up on the way.

As he walked up to the door, another couple did as well.

"They're closed?" the woman asked, puzzled.

Max slid his P.I. license from his pocket and flashed it.

"Health inspector," he said. "There seem to be some issues. They should have them cleared up soon."

"What kind of issues?"

Max lowered his voice and leaned in. "Roaches."

"Eww!" she shrieked. Her date pulled her away.

"We'll go somewhere else," he reassured her.

"I'm not hungry anymore," she said. "I want to go home."

The man scowled at Max, but he just smiled back.

As they walked away, the door to the restaurant opened. "Mr. Boucher, come in," a voice said. "We've been expecting you."

Well, the method of approach had been determined for him. So much for subtle or storming.

Chapter Twelve

"Max, is it?"

"I'd prefer you call me Mr. Boucher, at least for now."

"Certainly. Have a seat."

The interior of the restaurant was dimly lit. Dishes clattered, as bus staff cleared tables clearly intended for use this evening, now empty.

"Something to eat? Drink?"

"I'm okay for now."

"Whiskey usually, though, correct?"

"You know me well."

"Pour Mr. Boucher some Yamazaki," the slim man said, snapping his fingers.

"I said I was fine."

"I want you to try this one. It isn't 'Scotch' per se, but an excellent Japanese alternative. Sherry cask. Your preference, no?"

"Okay." Max looked around. "What do you want, exactly?"

"Just to talk," he said. A rotund waiter showed up with two glasses, and an interesting looking bottle. A bucket of ice followed.

"Straight or rocks?"

"Straight for me." Max answered.

Dropping three ice cubes into his own glass, the man across from him poured two fingers into each.

"To business," he said, raising his glass.

Max hesitated.

"You saw me pour, Mr. Boucher. Your glass is no different from mine."

"I'm just not sure I want to drink to business with you."

"Understandable. Still..."

Max sniffed the liquid in the glass. Floral, citrus like.

Not exactly his usual highland, but after a tentative sip he approved.

"Not bad," he said. "You've cleared your restaurant, and I assume you had me followed just so we could have this conversation?"

The Asian nodded.

"You seem to know who I am. But I don't think I caught your name."

"Myung Yong. The pleasure is mine." The small man bowed his head slightly.

Max noted that he wore all black, as did all of his staff. His shirt appeared to be silk. In the middle, he wore a gold pin the others did not with a large ruby in the center.

His pants were of a similar material but looked heavier that the shirt. His feet were in slippers Max had only seen in martial arts movies.

"Max Boucher, to make it official," Max held out his hand.

The other man took it and shook. His skin was smooth, but Max felt callouses on his knuckles.

A fighter, perhaps.

"What can I do for you Mr. Yong?"

"Perhaps it is what I can do for you."

"Do you have a lead for me on the case of the missing dogs in Queen Anne?"

"Wasn't the original dog you were hired to find returned today?"

"How would you know?"

"You have aroused my interest, Max." The man drug out his name, elongated it somehow.

"Good to have a fan," Max answered.

A smile tugged at the corner of the man's mouth, but he simply gestured for him to continue.

"One dog was returned, yes. To the woman who initially hired me."

"Then you are finished with your case?"

"Not hardly. She hired me on behalf of other owners missing pets as well. They were able to raise a tidy sum." Max leaned back, studying the man's reaction.

The Asian's smile did not falter. In fact, it may have widened a little. "What is a tidy sum?"

"I'd hate to say."

"What if I have another case for you?"

"Depending on how much work it is, I may be able to handle both at the same time," Max answered. "Why don't you share the details with me?"

"You would have to agree to work for me exclusively during the time I employ you."

"Afraid I can't do that," Max said, after pausing as if he was considering the offer. "I have several cases at the moment."

"Cut-the-bull-shit," the man hissed. "I know more of your affairs than you might like Max. That house in Queen Anne, the one you don't live in, gets rather expensive doesn't it?"

Max stood. "This conversation seems to have turned less than friendly. My house, and my finances are none of your goddamn business. You want to hire me? You do it on my terms."

"You think I have something to do with the disappearance of these dogs, Max?" The Asian was a full head shorter than he was but stood chest to chest with him anyway.

"I do," Max said. "That's why I came here."

"That is a very personal accusation."

"It is very personal when my friends' dogs disappear. When dog body parts appear on my partner's door when I'm there for dinner. When I find a dog, I am looking for in the dog park where he was taken, clearly injured."

"Why you not ask me?" the man said, his English slipping as his anger rose.

"Ask you?"

"Yes. Ask, Mr. Boucher."

Max had taken martial arts in the Marines, and had no fear of scrapping, and he'd perfected his art further as a cop. He could hold his own, if need be.

This guy looked like he lived them though. His stance, his bearing told Max he would be fast. And his punches and kicks would be efficient, hard.

And painful.

"I do have a few questions," Max said, spreading his hands wide. "Maybe we got off on the wrong foot."

"Indeed." The other man relaxed, bowing. "I apologize for my reaction. Please." Yong gestured at the seat Max had just vacated.

Max sat and drained the whiskey in one gulp.

"Another?" his host asked, sitting as well.

"Certainly," he said, and the man poured.

"Go ahead, ask what you want."

"This might be offensive, but I'm just going to relate what I have heard."

"Fine."

"I am not a cop, remember. I'm just a P.I. Nothing you say here has to go beyond these walls."

"Mr. Boucher, perhaps you do not understand our culture. Honor is most important. I will answer what I can."

"Are you a part of any illegal activities? A friend at the police department—"

"Your old partner, Tony."

"My old partner, yes. He led me to believe you may be a part of the Korean mafia, a member of the Chijon family."

"I have never heard of such a thing. There are those from my country who engage in illegal activities, even in cooperation with others, but I am not a part of those, and I would hardly call their organization mafia."

"You rescued many dogs who needed homes, from shelters and other organizations. They were never seen again."

"Of course not. I found homes for them."

"But not locally."

"No. Not locally."

"When you were asked to provide information on where they went, you declined."

"I did. It is my right, correct?"

"It is. But then the shelters stopped allowing you to rescue animals."

"That was most unfortunate."

"Where are the dogs, Mr. Yong?"

"Homes, with many people all over."

"The recent disappearances?"

"You mean your case in Queen Anne?"

"And others."

"Others?"

"All over the city. Seems Queen Anne is only a part of something larger."

"This is most disturbing," his host said, getting up and starting to pace.

"Disturbing?"

"Yes."

"Care to explain what you mean by that?"

"No, I will not."

Max sighed. "Then I'm afraid we're done here."

"You do not wish to hear about my case?"

"If it is exclusive, and I cannot work on other things at the same time, then no." Max stood.

"I know why this case has you so in-ter-est-ed." The Asian emphasized every syllable of the last word.

"Really? Why would that be?" Max asked.

"Your dog, who is so much a part of your own case. You lost yours, you cannot bear to other owners suffer."

Max blinked. "Perhaps."

"Today, a dog named Jennifer returned, and that affected you, didn't it?"

Max said nothing.

"You don't have to say anything. Just the name. Jenny."

"You seem to know a lot about me, Mr. Yong. You want to tell me how, and why now, when I am on this case?"

"It is not this case which interests me."

"What is it then?"

"Your *missing* wife."

Emphasis on missing. Not dead. Not like everyone else, who never used either word, but implied the second.

"You can keep chasing dogs, Mr. Boucher. You can be a pet detective, maybe even solve this one, or you can do something for me far more lucrative."

"What would that have to do with my wife?" Max said. He tried to keep the menace from his voice but heard it.

Felt his hands clench and unclench in fists.

Fists he intended to use, consequence be damned.

"My daughter is missing," Mr. Yong said. "I think you are the man who can find her."

***

Max sat back down. Hard.

Grabbed the bottle. Poured his own whiskey.

In the neighborhood of four fingers and a thumb. In fact, he just filled the fucking glass.

Mr. Yong sat across from him.

"Do I have your attention now?"

"Talk," Max said. His teeth were clenched. The word was all he could manage.

"My daughter is not missing in the way of your wife. She ran away."

"What does that have to do with me?"

"She ran away, Mr. Boucher. But her intentional disappearance may relate to your wife's unintentional one."

"What makes you say that?"

"I am a powerful..." Mr. Yong paused. "I have friends. I have kept an eye on her, to assure myself she remains safe."

"I see," Max said. He took a large swallow of whiskey.

"She has fallen into the wrong crowd, a filthy industry."

Max stayed silent.

"They also take women against their will for their own purposes."

"You think they took my wife?" Max asked.

"They are the type of people who could have."

"So, you have no evidence. Not even a real suspicion. You're trying to play on my past for sympathy, to elicit my help, for what?"

"I want you to bring my daughter back."

"Against her will?"

"That's why the police won't help."

"And in trade? Other than my usual fee, you will help me try to find my wife?"

Mr. Yong nodded.

"How about this?" Max stood, draining his glass. "How about you shove that up your ass."

"What?"

"I ain't gonna go drag your daughter back to you, no matter what you pay. Not if she doesn't want to come. I don't do that for any price."

"That—"

"Shut up. You are investigating me, following me, using my past to manipulate me, I don't like it. As a result, I don't like you."

"So, you are telling me no?"

"I am. I'm telling you to stay away from me, and my case."

"That is a decision you will regret." As he stood, Max pulled his .45.

"Sit. Tell your goons to do the same." Yong gestured, and his men sat.

"I'm leaving. I'm not going to see you again. If I do, I'll come back here. I have friends too. I'd hate for them to find anything illegal going on here."

"You will be sorry you said that," Yong said.

"Maybe," Max replied. "Time will tell, but you and I are done."

He backed toward the door.

"I'll see you around," Yong said.

"Not if I see you coming first," Max replied.

He reached the door and eased his way out.

On the sidewalk were two couples, looking at the closed sign with puzzled expressions.

"How come they are closed?" they asked him.

"They'll reopen soon," Max said, holstering his weapon. "As soon as they get rid of the rats."

He didn't wait for a response but turned and walked past them.

He walked the two blocks to the Buick, feeling the whole time as if he was being watched.

It couldn't be Yong or his men, at least he didn't think so.

Still, he glanced around, looking for movement, someone unusual in the crowd. There was nothing other than his gut instinct.

Reaching his car, he unlocked the door, and slid into the driver's seat with a final look around.

Something hit him in the back of the head, hard.

Max fell forward onto the wheel. A second blow followed, and the lights went out.

Chapter Thirteen

Odd shapes populated the inside of his eyelids.
Instinct made Max squeeze them shut tighter.
He tried to move. Found his arms secured somehow, over his head.
Some experimentation revealed his legs were also secured, his feet close together.
Cold bit into his skin, a damp cold. This time of year, that meant it was evening. By the chill, late evening.
He could smell the sound. You could tell almost any location in Seattle by some kind of local smell. Big cities all had them: exhaust, trash, restaurants or varying ethnicity, even trees or flowers in bloom.
Near the bay, those all took a back seat, and a longtime resident could sense it, simply by smell.
His feet were bare. Unfortunate, due to the cold, but he stretched out his toes. Rough concrete covered in dirt met them.
The figures still danced in his vision, and he knew opening his eyes would be painful, at least at first.
But he felt the need to discover his surroundings and find out where he was being held.
He tried to remember how he got here but couldn't. The last thing he remembered was a sharp blow to the back of his head, two actually.
Mentally, he searched for a wound. Turned his head and found it.

Delayed opening his eyes, until the sharp pain from just above his right temple dissipated.

Someone had been waiting for him in his back seat.

Not Yong, but maybe someone he'd hired. That seemed unlikely.

Yong had really seemed convinced he would hire Max, take him off one case, put him on another, and get rid of him that way.

Sure, he'd been upset Max had rejected his offer, but why?

Yong felt wrong for the role of a mastermind. Minion maybe.

Max opened his eyes. Light stabbed at the retinas, and he closed them again, blinked, and opened them. The throbbing over his temple intensified.

The room revealed was small and rough. It felt like a closet, and brooms, mop buckets, and a floor buffer with a frayed cord told him it was likely a janitor's.

Funny that the room holding the cleaning supplies was filthy. Dirt on the floor, cobwebs in the corner, and a really bright bulb hanging in the center on a chain.

It swung with an unseen breeze, and shadows danced in the corners.

There was a window, high up on the wall, long and skinny.

Max tested his restraints. Around his wrists they were almost comfortable, though tight. Preparing himself for the pain he knew would come from his head, he looked up.

He'd seen the movies, but the leather buckled around his wrists still took him by surprise. It appeared to be lined with white cloth of some kind, padding perhaps.

They were the kind of restraints used in a hospital, or a mental institution.

The kind to protect the patient from himself and protect the staff.

The light went out, and the door opened.

"Hello Mr. Boucher," a sultry female voice said.

Max tried to speak. Found his mouth filled with cotton. Thirst suddenly became a priority. *How long had he been out?*

"Don't talk," the voice said. "Don't be concerned, either. You will not be here for long. Some of my guests have had a much longer stay."

Max swallowed. Desperately tried to clear his throat. He wanted to respond.

"I know of your need to express yourself. I even sympathize. The timing of our conversation is, however, no accident."

"Wha—" he coughed, swore there must be glass in his throat, trying to cut it open from the inside.

"What do I want?" the woman said. "That, Max, is a long list."

Something familiar in her tone tried to produce a memory and failed.

"But for the moment, from you, what I want is for you to stop sniffing around, so to speak."

He was not gagged and managed to spit some of the glass onto the floor. The dark kept him from determining the color, but he figured out he must not be dying.

"People's pets are missing. So what. Tell your clients to adopt new ones. Leave this alone."

The copper taste he swallowed told him there was blood in his mouth. He was unsure where it had come from, but it was definitely there. Still, he tried to speak through the fire, with no success.

"Your insane curiosity, the thing that makes you a great detective, can also get you into painful positions."

From the darkness, he heard a whoosh. Knew what it meant. Tightened his muscles, with no other method to protect himself.

Something struck his ribs, left side.

The object was long, thin, and hard. The blow stung.

A grunt escaped his throat. He swallowed again. Tried to speak.

"It's more than just dehydration, Max, although the effects will wear off soon. In fact, I'm not sure exactly the effect it will have on you. It works very well at keeping dogs quiet."

He grunted. Progress, but not words. Not yet.

"I brought you here for only one reason, Max. To show you I can. We can. We can reach out and touch you. Take you, just like a dog and put you in a cage."

He didn't understand what kept him from speaking. From what the woman was saying, it must be a drug of some sort.

"If you are too much trouble, we can put you down Max. That might bring attention we don't really want. I certainly don't think you want that, do you?"

Max struggled against the restraints.

He couldn't see. His arms ached, his throat was raw, disabling his voice.

He wanted to scream, find a way to get free.

"Let this be a warning, Max. Shall we call it a friendly one?"

He struggled more. Squinted his eyes shut with the effort. Felt his left foot move. Not enough to escape, but it moved.

"Time to get back now, Max."

He struggled, and then felt a needle enter his tricep. He tried to flex and resist.

"Oh, now that's going to leave a mark."

He felt a sting as liquid pushed into his veins.

"Good night, Max," the voice said.

A second later, he felt his chin hit his chest, then nothing.

***

His phone rang.

He grumbled. Didn't I shut that off? He had, last he remembered.

Max's throat was full of gravel. Head ached. Ribs ached.

"Just a minute," he said, working to get his eyes open. When he finally managed to overcome the weight of the lids, he found himself in the back seat of his car.

Tried to sit up, and instead rolled onto the floor, got stuck in the narrow space between the seats. Struggled to get free. His phone was still ringing.

Where was it?

There. On the front seat, passenger side.

He'd had a dream. A dream of being trapped in a closet. Interrogated.

Why the hell had he slept in his car?

Max reached for the phone, fighting the pounding headache at his temple.

When he saw a wide red mark across his wrist, he stopped and lifted his right hand to his head.

The tricep ached where he remembered someone putting a needle.

Gingerly, he reached for his temple, and the pain there exploded when he discovered a large goose egg.

It wasn't a dream.

Max groaned out loud.

"Can I talk?" he asked the empty car and heard his own voice as an answer.

It sounded horrible.

The phone stopped ringing. Thank God.

Next to it was a bottle of water. Max grabbed it and drained it.

Felt the need for a morning piss.

Was it morning?

Looked out the window. Looked like it. Gray, low clouds. Just enough light to be dawn.

Reaching for the phone using his left hand, he picked it up and looked at the time.

8:22, must be a.m. The battery said 22%, and he was sure it had been lower when he shut the phone off—when? Several hours ago, when he was headed into Yong's.

He leaned the seat forward and struggled to reach for the door handle on the driver's side.

A tap sounded on the passenger window.

Standing there was a cop, holding a nightstick. He scowled and made a 'roll-the-window-down' motion.

Max pointed to the driver's door. The cop shook his head. Fuck.

He slid over and could feel the cop watching him. Leaned the passenger seat forward too.

It gave the interior of the coupe an odd look, like the backs of two people were bowed low in prayer.

Max leaned forward, grabbed the window crank, and with some effort and pain, lowered the glass.

"You can't sleep in your car here," the cop said.

Thanks, Captain Obvious, Max thought.

Out loud he said, "Thanks officer. Rough night last night. I won't let it happen again."

The officer looked over the car with a disapproving glance. "You got any I.D.?"

"Certainly," he said, and reached for his wallet, mildly surprised when he found it.

"Do it slow," the cop said, unbuckling the strap on his holster.

Jesus. You'd get shot now for breathing sideways. Max understood, but still hated it.

He struggled to pull it from his back pocket and offered his driver's license.

"Max Boucher?" the guy asked.

"That's me."

"The former detective?"

"Yep," Max said. Great, either a fan or a hater. He really only had two audiences in the police department.

"What the hell are you doing here? I heard you were a private dick now. That true?"

"I am," Max said. Each word still tore through his throat, and he still had to pee, a need that grew more urgent every passing moment.

"What happened?" the uniform said, pointing at his head.

"Long story. Listen, I could use a hand here."

"What can I do for you, Detective?"

Good. He was a fan.

"First of all, I need to piss something awful, and then I could use some water and coffee, in that order."

The cop reached in the window, and popped the lock, opening the door.

"Pisser is right over there," he said, pointing.

Max found he was at the dog park. Public restrooms were not far away.

His car was in the middle of the parking lot, parked crooked and taking up two spaces.

The lot was rapidly filling with early morning dog walkers and joggers who used the nearby trails.

"I'll keep an eye on your car," the cop said.

"Thanks," Max said, jogging over to take care of nature's call.

He entered the restroom quickly and welcomed relief with closed eyes.

When he finished, he opened them.

In front of him, on the wall, written in sharpie, were the words:

For a doggone good time, Call Max!

His number was scrawled underneath.

He washed his hands and walked back to his car.

The cop was standing, talking on what appeared to be Max's phone.

"I'll tell him," he said, and ended the call. He handed it back to Max.

"It rang, so I answered," the cop said. "It was a Dr. Gamble. She asked you to come to her clinic right away."

"Damn!" Max swore.

He couldn't catch a break.

Running around to the driver's door, he hoped the keys were there.

Hoped the good Doctor had water, and coffee.

"Hey!" the cop said, leaning down to the still open passenger window. "You owe me a story."

"Give me a call, and I'll share sometime," Max said. He tossed a card to the cop, who picked it up.

Max leaned over and rolled up the window. It was cool this morning.

He fired up the motor and headed for Dr. Gamble's office.

What now? he wondered.

***

Max pulled into the street where the vet clinic was.

There were three police cruisers parked on the street.

He found a spot, with some difficulty, about half a block away, and walked back.

When he got near the door, a uniformed officer stopped him.

"Sorry sir, crime scene."

"They're expecting me," he said. "Max Boucher."

The patrolman turned and spoke into a radio. A moment later, he said. "Go ahead."

"Thanks," Max said, walking inside.

There was no evidence of a crime on the stoop, and as he entered the door, two patrolmen were preparing to leave. A detective, by the worn suit, stood next to Dr. Gamble, jotting something in a notebook.

He looked up, and Max recognized him. "Hi Chris," he said.

The older man had been in robbery/homicide before the two departments had both become a part of major crimes and split into their own departments. Now Detective Sparks worked robbery. He was good.

"Max!" the man's face lit up. "How have you been?"

"Good," Max said, shaking his hand. "How about you?"

"Doing well. Haven't seen you around."

"The life of a private dick is busy."

"Maybe I will try it myself in a few years," Chris said.

"What's going on here?" Max asked.

"Someone broke in," Dr. Gamble said. "But didn't take the usual stuff."

"What did they take?" he asked.

"They took medical records. All of the canine ones."

"What?"

"That's what I said," Sparks replied. "Makes no sense at all."

"Except in light of my investigation."

"Tell him the rest," Chris instructed the vet.

"They put a bug on my computer. Deleted all the EMR data."

"EMR?"

"Electronic Medical Records. Most people think of them in relation to people, but vets use them too. Paperless office. Saves money and offers owners better security too."

"Security?"

"Breeders would pay big money to get a look at some records. But this wasn't a theft of the records."

"They just deleted them?" he asked. "What could have been in them?"

"Maybe a clue to why someone has targeted these particular dogs," she said.

Max shook his head. This was nuts.

He didn't even think the dogs were targeted that specifically.

"When did this happen?"

"Around 5 a.m. we think. The odd part is, another vet was hit last night as well. Same thing."

"Let me guess. That office treated some of the missing dogs as well?"

"You must be Sherlock," Sparks joked.

"Not the first time that one has been used on me lately," Max said. "It's getting old."

"Fine. What is your theory then?"

"I have no idea."

"And what happened to your head?"

"Long story."

"Related to this?" the detective gestured.

"I don't think so," Max lied. Sherlock. Lying. Some things were starting to become patterns.

"Fine. Well, let me know if you come up with anything." Chris snapped his notebook shut.

Max could fool a lot of people, but certainly not all the cops he was surrounded by.

"Thanks. You too." They shook hands.

"I'll let you know if I think of a motive," Dr. Gamble said.

"Sure," Detective Sparks said, looking the two of them over. "Have a nice day."

He left.

"He seemed kind of pissed at you," Jerri said.

"He knew I was lying about my head," Max said. "Like any cop, he doesn't like to be lied to. He also thinks we are both hiding something. Together."

"How do you figure?" she asked.

"The way he looked at us before he left. Are you gonna tell me?"

"Tell you what?"

"What you hid from the detective. And why."

"Max—"

"Enough!" he cut her off. "I went through shit last night, and learned damn near zilch, except I think at least two people want me off this case, with two totally different motives, and I don't know what either of them are. No matter what the fee, it would be a hell of a lot easier just to walk away from this. Talk."

"There were dogs in the kennels last night, in for various reasons. A couple were just in to be fixed. They came in late, so I kept them overnight for the owners."

"And?"

"All the dogs were out of their kennels when I got here. The cop asked me to make sure they were all here."

"But they weren't." Max made it a statement.

"No. The two healthiest ones are missing. And the records are a bigger deal than you think, than the cops think."

"Why is that?"

"Owner's names, addresses, pet age and breeds. A database of dogs to take."

"You said they destroyed them."

"They took physical copies, what ones there were, but I would bet they copied the EMR before they deleted it."

"What makes you say that?"

"I would. But it would have to be someone who knew the system. It is pretty well protected."

"Any ideas?" Max asked.

"I might have at least come up with a possible motive."

"What would that be?"

"Organ harvesting."

"You mean like for transplants?"

"Could be. It would make sense. Healthy dogs. They never come back."

"Would they kill them when they are done?"

"Sometimes. But they wouldn't have to. They could find them other homes, through shelters elsewhere."

"Aren't many of the dogs chipped?"

"If you mean the ownership chips, yes, but they can be removed, or more easily, reprogrammed, again by someone who knows the system."

"Is this big business?"

"Getting more popular, especially with the rise of pet health insurance."

"Insurance pays for it."

"The big companies get stuck with the bill. Mom and pop American get their dog back, healthy. The other pup is sent off, probably a good sympathy rescue. Only has one kidney, missing a piece of liver, something like that."

"And if they die on the table, no one knows."

"Way easier source than legal channels. Pets acting as organ donors isn't exactly popular yet, although the numbers are rising."

"Just not fast enough."

"Not fast enough for someone."

"How much are we talking about here?"

"Depends on the dog, the organ, whether they can take more than one from the same animal."

"Ball park?"

"Ten grand, maybe more."

"Wow. Why mutts?"

"They make better donors, like the article I showed you said. Their organs are less likely to be rejected."

You think this is it?"

"It makes the most sense."

"So why are there two people, or groups trying to stop my investigation?"

"Eliminate the competition, maybe."

"That doesn't feel right."

"Well, that part is for you to figure out."

"So where do we go from here?"

"Well, I didn't tell the cops one other thing."

"What's that?"

"I have a backup of the EMR, and an idea how to prove my theory."

"How would that be?"

"Vets aren't as organized yet as people doctors, but there is a loose national database."

"I love you, Dr. Gamble," Max said, then stopped.

Even in a friendly, platonic way, he hadn't said those words to anyone in three years.

Not since he'd last said them to Jenny, the morning he left for work, and returned to find her missing.

"What's wrong?" she asked.

Max swallowed and pasted a smile on his face. "Goose walked over my grave, that's all. Let's get to work." Another repeated expression.

Dr. Gamble led him to a safe in the wall, where she pulled out a small portable hard drive, brought it over and plugged it into her laptop.

"Let me get you some coffee," she said.

Max watched the squat, older woman walk away, and wondered if he might be healing after all.

He hoped not.

HARVESTED

Chapter Fourteen

Not averse to technology, Max jumped right in. Or tried to.

He rapidly discovered he had a lot to learn about the medical field, even in the world of veterinary medicine.

He also learned that people were more serious about their dogs than he ever had been, maybe to his detriment.

People had insurance for their dogs, very similar to the health insurance they had for themselves. It not only covered major medical, but covered wellness visits, teeth cleaning, and other routine exams, in some cases even included grooming.

There were pet chiropractors, specialty surgeons, DNA labs, breeding consultants, and more.

The business was huge.

Not only that, but there had been major strides in pet medicine directly related to progress in human medicine. Hip and knee replacements were common, and an up and coming trend was organ transplants.

Max was amazed, yet strangely pleased. Even growing up, he'd always thought of pets like family.

Hell, sometimes they were even better than family.

The EMR system was elaborate and filled with details. Even though not every vet had adopted it, if Dr. Gamble was to be believed, there were over 7500 dogs listed in Seattle alone. The records from her office contained nearly 400 animals, over half of them dogs.

He was investigating a couple dozen missing from Queen Anne.

The doctor's notes were often extensive. Pet diet, habits, where they walked, and even where they lived.

He found they were not that easy to navigate. You almost had to know the system to find the relevant information.

The data was not available online, and local copies would be the only way to get it. Vets were not yet harvesting the power of cloud computing, but according to Jerri it might be just around the corner. Because of her back up, she could warn the owners of her patients. She could let other vets know about the theft and tell them to be vigilant about their records.

Max learned all this, and more, in a few short hours.

The most significant find was how inefficient the national database was.

Placing chips in animals and adding the data to a national list helped vets find dogs and return them to their owners. But there was no way to search the database for dogs reported missing. Numbers were solid for dogs found, and some information could be assumed from that, but nothing definitive.

"Not all owners report dogs missing to vets and local clinics. Many just check local shelters and dog catchers. Essentially law enforcement. When a vet reunites a dog and its owner, it is often luck more than anything else," Dr. Gamble explained.

"Hell, I didn't even know this system existed." Max said.

"Public education has been poor," she said. "Because the system is ineffective. Of course, a big reason it is ineffective is because the public doesn't know about it. Even when a dog is reported missing to a vet, they don't always input the data right away. Runaways and hit and run situations are all too common. It is kind of like the electronic medical records system. Even people doctors were reluctant to adopt it. It's better, but it is one more new thing to learn. In rural areas, its use is even rarer," Dr. Gamble told him.

"So why take dogs from a city, where its use is more common?"

"One of the reason rural vets don't use the system is they know all of their patients. A smaller practice means a more intimate connection to the community.

"I know my regulars. Recognize them, and their owners, even on the street. But the ones who come infrequently for shots and nothing more? If they never came back in, I wouldn't know unless I looked."

"Do you look?"

"Rarely. I am more that busy enough with the regulars who do show up."

"You send out reminders?"

"The computer does. By e-mail, and even reminders for staff to print mail. But I don't look at them, and the staff doesn't really either. We send them and get about 30% response. That's pretty good, actually, compared to others."

"So how did you know about the dogs missing in Queen Anne?"

"Helen. She let all the area vets know right away. Since most of them are my patients, she focused on me and my practice."

"There could be more of your patients missing outside Helen's little circle?"

"Easily."

"Any way to check?"

"Not an efficient one. We could call every dog owner on the list."

"Not sure we have time. I need to share this with the police. Not that they will do anything about it, but it won't hurt."

"Fine Max," she said. As he stood up from his seat near her desk, and stretched, she wrapped her arms around him and hugged him.

Surprised, at first, he did nothing. Then he hugged her back, a gentle, quick squeeze before he moved away and activated his phone.

"Detective Delato," Tony answered.

"Hey, it's Max."

"I was about to call and check on you. What's up?"

"Who do I need to talk to about new information relating to my case?"

"Related to the burglary?"

"You heard?"

"You know Detective Sparks."

"Yeah. More related to the dogs themselves. We have a theory."

"We?"

"Dr. Gamble and I."

"Spill it. Then I'll put you in touch with Animal Crimes."

Max explained, and at the end Tony whistled. "Why don't you come down and tell them in person. I'd like to see you anyway."

"You got it," Max said, looking at his watch. "I'll be there around 2."

***

There were two groups trying to stall his investigation.

A spirited talk at a restaurant came from one, being knocked out, restrained, and threatened came from another. But which one was responsible for the burglaries? And why had Yong seemed so uncomfortable?

"That's unfortunate," he'd said.

Neither side was a part of the good guys. Or so he believed. A theory gave them a motive. But what if he was wrong?

What if each group had their own motives? Organ harvesting seemed valid from what Dr. Gamble said, but what was the other? Or were the two working together, just from different angles?

Could the enemy of his enemy be his friend in this case?

He thought of Yong. Then of the closet and being restrained.

Who was who?

Maybe he should go ask.

Before he had time to reconsider, before he even thought of another alternative, Max resolved to do just that.

"Dr. Gamble?" he called across the room.

She looked up from her desk, where she had been studying the records as they reloaded.

"I'm going to lunch. You want me to bring you back anything?"

"Where are you going?" she asked.

"Yong's," he said.

"You like that place? No thanks, I'll grab something a little while later."

"Suit yourself," he said, waving as he left the building.

***

On the way to Yong's, Max stopped and got a phone charger for his car at a convenience store. He removed the cigarette lighter and plugged it in. He hadn't been home it what seemed like forever, and his prospects for a good night's sleep and a solid overnight charge for his phone seemed slim.

Yong's was busy, in stark contrast to the night before. The restaurant clearly had a large lunch following, and they hadn't known he was coming this time.

As he walked toward the door, his phone rang. He answered without thinking.

"Boucher."

"Max, it's Tony. I thought you were coming over."

"I was. Something came up. I'll be there a little later this afternoon."

"The guy you should talk to is leaving for the day soon."

"How about tomorrow morning then?"

"You okay, Max?"

"Never better. Just have something to take care of."

"If you say so. Talk tomorrow."

This time, when he entered the front door, a host greeted him.

"Just you for lunch?" the man asked.

Fuck you, Max thought. It's been just me for lunch for the last three years.

Out loud, he said, "Yes."

"The bar okay?"

When he looked over and saw that Myung Yong was tending, Max nodded.

"Perfect," he said, and followed the man over to an empty stool.

"To drink?" he asked.

"Yamazaki straight," he replied. The host turned to the bartender and froze. Yong stood staring at Max.

"Hi there," Max said. "I'd like to get in a late lunch. Then if you're free, can we talk?"

"Sure," Yong replied. "Let me get your drink, on the house."

Max smiled, and spun on his barstool, watching the room.

"What can I get you to eat?" a young, pretty waitress asked.

"Kimchi jjigae," Max said.

The youngster blinked at his pronunciation and decisiveness. "Anything else?" she asked, pen poised to write.

"That's all—for now," Max said.

"I'll get this started right away."

Max turned back to the bar to find his drink had arrived, and Yong was busily serving other customers.

Max sipped while waiting for his food to arrive. Yong glanced at him from time to time, but paid him no special attention, or at least didn't appear to.

As he sat at the bar, Max watched the other patrons, but none seemed to take an undue interest in him. When his food arrived, he dug in, watching as the lunch crowd thinned, and the barstools emptied.

The stew was good. Really good.

HARVESTED

Chapter Fifteen

"Have you changed your mind, Mr. Boucher?"

"Depends" Max said. "I do have some questions."

"What makes you think I will answer?"

"I have a proposition for you."

"What happened to your head?" Yong appeared nervous.

There was a mirror over the bar, and Max could see shadows behind him. The restaurant was emptying, the lull before the dinner rush, but there were several men watching the two of them.

"I thought maybe you knew."

"How would I?"

"If you don't, then someone else also wants me off this case. I have the feeling the two of you might know each other."

"What makes you think so?"

"Two people, entirely unrelated, want me to drop an investigation. How stupid do you think I am?"

"Not stupid. American stubborn. Not stupid."

"First question. The bit with your daughter? Bullshit or fact?"

"Fact," Yong said. "She is—"

Max cut him off with a raised hand. Drained his whiskey and asked for another. When it was poured, he continued.

"Fact is enough for now. How about the rest?"

"What you mean?"

"You can play dumb if you want Yong. I'll walk out, and you won't see me again, except as we discussed last night."

"Why are you here?"

"You have no fucking clue about my wife, but I do about your daughter. My daughter died, you know?"

Yong nodded.

"Father to father? I wish every day she was still here. Be happy yours is still alive. Of course, I sympathize."

"Thank you," Yong said with a bow.

"Yeah, except here's the thing," Max drained his current glass of whiskey. His head felt a little fogged, but he intended to clear it really soon.

Standing abruptly, he grabbed Yong's collar, pulling him close.

"You don't use my wife or kid as leverage, ever again. You got something to say? Something you want me to do for you? Then fucking say it."

A second later he found himself spinning, and landed, on his back on the top of the bar. Yong now held his collar.

"You come in my place of business; you threaten me. What're you really doing here, Boucher?"

Max grabbed the smaller man, and spun him over the bar, sliding off after him. Standing, he adopted a boxer's stance, and faced Yong, who had also landed on his feet.

"You really want to fight me?" Max said. "Go ahead, you little fuck. Give it your best shot. Your martial arts shit might kick my ass, but I guarantee I will get some licks in first."

"This not the way to get my cooperation," Yong said.

"Nor mine," Max said. "Want to quit this shit, and talk? Or you wanna dance?"

A part of him hoped the little man really wanted to fight. Max was looking for an outlet for his frustration, and this would do nicely.

On the other hand, he wanted answers. Sympathy father to father be damned.

If he had to go drag Yong's daughter back here to get them, so be it. She'd probably run off again anyway, but at least he'd feel like he'd done his part.

That sounded cold, he thought.

"I don't want to fight you Boucher," Yong said, bowing. "Let's talk instead."

"Okay," Max said, lowering his fists. "But not like last night."

"Yes," Yong said, guarded.

"You gotta tell me the truth," Max said.

"I will do what I can," Yong replied. He gestured to a booth, and Max sat across from him.

The young waitress reappeared and set glasses in front of them.

Max hardly touched his. He'd had enough to drink. It wasn't even five o'clock yet.

"Tell me about the dogs, Yong," he started.

To his surprise, the man across from him began to sob.

***

Max had no idea what to do. Where to put his hands.

He looked down at his drink and took a sip after all, waiting.

"Excuse me," Yong said, and disappeared.

Max took the time to really look around the restaurant. Standard tables and booths padded wooden chairs, yet the decorations spoke of some wealth.

What appeared to be original art hung on the walls in this section, and the bar itself was magnificent. The cabinet behind it held several mirrors with designs in each corner. Carvings of dragons and other unidentifiable figures protruded from the shelves holding the bottles.

A quick perusal told him much of the liquor was top shelf.

When Yong returned a few moments later, he was completely recovered.

"My apologies," he said. "I usually do not display such emotion."

"I want to understand, Mr. Yong," Max said. 'But honestly, after last evening, I don't feel terribly warm towards you and your associates."

"For that, I also apologize Mr. Boucher." Yong's tone was much more formal.

"Thanks," Max said.

"I will be honest with you, Mr. Boucher."

"Call me Max."

"Yes. Max." Using his first name was clearly awkward for Yong. "I thought I was doing the right thing by rescuing dogs."

"And now?"

"After your—visit—last night, I did some checking. I should have believed my daughter."

"Your daughter? I'm not sure I understand."

"I work with certain—associates who have needs from time to time."

"I'm not the police," Max said.

"I meet those needs for certain compensation," Yong continued as if Max had never spoken. "One of them approached me about a year ago about a project, for which I would supply him dogs, supposedly for immigrant Korean families, who are often passed over by rescues and other normal channels."

"Why is that?"

"The perception is that Koreans eat dogs."

"And do you?"

"Some of our people do, but few regularly, and rarely in the United States. Much of our society frowns on the practice."

"Then they were supposed to be pets?"

He nodded.

"What did your daughter say?"

"She told me they were being used as organ donors for other dogs."

"You didn't believe her?"

"My associates assured me otherwise when I approached them."

"Is that why she left?"

"Among other things. She was rebelling anyway. She does not agree with some of our cultural practices."

"So why tell me this now?"

"Will it help your investigation?"

"I have no idea. Can you give me names?"

"No. If I give you more, they will know the source. It will put my other business ventures at risk."

"Alright. What do you want from me?"

"Can you give my daughter a message for me?"

"I can try."

"That is all I can ask. I will give you an address."

"What's the message?"

Yong handed him an envelope.

"Is there more you can give me?"

Yong handed him another envelope. "This one is for you."

Max started to open it.

"Not here," Yong said. "And I fear I must apologize to you again, Mr. Boucher."

"For what?"

"You cannot be seen walking out the front door. The impression that would create would be—unfortunate."

"No problem. I can slip out the back."

"I am afraid that might be noticed as well," Yong said.

Something heavy and hard crashed into the back of Max's head, and he fell towards the floor, darkness closing in.

Not again, he thought. Then nothing.

HARVESTED

Chapter Sixteen

A phone started ringing. It rang a few times, at least that he heard, and then stopped.

Why can't I ever remember to turn that thing down?

Max heard knocking. No, tapping, like on glass.

His head throbbed, and he tried to remember. Prying his eyes open, he saw the ceiling first, dome light in the center.

It would be so nice to wake up in his own bed, and not his car.

What the hell was he doing in his car?

Yong.

That bastard.

He sat up, and a light came through the side window, shone right into his eyes. The user of the flashlight pointed it off to the side, clearly scanning the rest of the interior. Then the beam darted outside. It illuminated a uniformed cop, who made a motion for him to roll down the window.

Squinting against the pain, Max sat up, and complied.

"Come here often?" the cop said.

"Not really," Max said. His mouth tasted like old blood.

"Funny, I swear I've seen you here before."

Max squinted again.

"Where am I?" he asked.

The cop directed the light around. The dog park at Queen Anne was revealed.

"Goddamn it!"

"Mr. Boucher, is it?"

"Yes," he told the cop.

"If you don't have a place to stay..."

"I own a house and have an apartment," Max growled.

"Then if you could go there..."

"I would love to," Max said. "What time is it?"

"Nine thirty. Listen, the park is technically closed, and I'm just trying to do my job, but if you need..."

"I don't need a thing," Max said.

Just then his phone started ringing again.

It sounded like an old telephone. Max had thought the ring tone was cool at first.

Now it got on his nerves. If the cop had not been blocking the window, he might have thrown the phone across the parking lot, something he'd done before, resulting in the purchase of a new phone.

In that way, he was thankful.

"Mind if I get that?" he asked the cop.

The man simply nodded, and Max answered.

"Max! It's Helen. I've been trying to reach you for hours."

"Sorry," he said, closing his eyes. "I have been tied up."

"Do you have anything new in the case?"

Her voice sounded loud. Much too loud. Max put the fingers of his right hand to his temple and winced as he found the original knot there. He could feel a second on the back of his head.

"I do. Listen, Helen, I am in a bit of a spot at the moment."

"Where are you?"

"The dog park."

"What are you doing there?"

"Long story."

"Why don't you come over?"

Max thought about it, thought of the alternatives, like a drive to Beacon Hill when he wasn't overly confident about his sobriety or his driving ability.

"Sure. Just give me a few moments, and I will stop by. Just two things."

"What's that?"

"Do you have any whiskey?"

"I stocked up after the last time you were here. I hope I have your brand."

"Good. How about ice?"

"Plenty of that. Max what's wrong?"

"I'll explain when I get there."

He ended the call. "Can I go now?" he asked the cop.

"Be my guest," the patrolman said. "Have a good night."

***

On the drive to Helen's Max noticed the Buick was getting low on gas.

How far had he driven? Or rather, had his car been driven. Twice he had woken up somewhere other than where he started.

He better remember to fill up before he attempted to go anywhere else.

Approaching Helen's door, he noticed the lights were on in her living room but looked dim.

It opened to reveal Helen, and her dog, who leapt around her feet.

"Hi Max, come on in," she said.

She was dressed in a rather fetching and what he perceived to be formal pantsuit. The material appeared to be smooth, either silk, or a close cousin. It was a dark blue and enhanced the blond woman's blue eyes. The dog twirled around his feet, tail wagging.

"Kennel," Helen said, and with a sad look the pup took off toward the rear of the house. Max was glad, in some ways.

He was just too tired to deal with the animal. Helen was another matter.

"What's the occasion?" he asked, swallowing hard.

"Nothing special," she said. "Why do you ask?"

He gestured to indicate her outfit.

"Oh, this old thing?" she gestured to her clothing and giggled. Then the laugh stopped. "What happened to your head?"

"Which time?" he asked, then answered himself. "Long story. I didn't ask about the ice for the drinks."

"Have you eaten?"

In answer, Max's stomach growled. The last thing he could remember eating was the kimchi jjigae at Yong's. That was what? Six, seven hours ago?

"Not lately. Last time was just before I got this," he pointed to the back of his head.

"Damn Max," she said. "You look like hell."

"Thanks."

"What happened?"

"How about that ice, and a drink first?"

Helen sat him down on her couch. The primary illumination in the room came from candles, making him certain she'd had something in mind other than discussing the case.

A few moments later, she emerged with a glass full of amber liquid, and an ice pack. She set the drink in front of him.

"Where do you want this?" she said, offering the ice. Using his right hand, Max gently applied it to the back of his head. Still, he saw stars.

With his left, he grabbed the glass, and took a sip.

"Hmm," he said. "What is this?"

"Chivas. The guy at the liquor store said it was good."

"It is," he lied, and set it aside. Some people loved that blend, but Max was pickier. He preferred his Scotch from higher on the shelves.

"So, tell me what you have so far," Helen said. She sat on the couch, close but facing him, her legs crossed in front of her.

Max elected to tell her a short version of the story, leaving out the part about the organ transplants.

"Then some of the dogs could still be alive?"

"Possibly. Although I have no clue where they might be."

"Not yet, right?"

"No, not yet."

From his pocket his phone rang. Max was starting to hate the device. He looked at the screen and saw it was Tony.

"Hey," he answered.

"You still coming in tomorrow?"

"Jesus, Tony, Thanks for the reminder. I completely forgot. I got—well, waylaid."

"You sound exhausted."

"Who's that?" Helen asked.

"Who's that?" Tony asked right after. "Are you with a woman, Max?"

"I'm at a client's house, Tony. It's a long story."

"I get it. Waylaid. Way to go, Max."

"It's not like that Tony. Not at all."

"Trudy will be so happy to hear you're feeling better."

"Tony—"

"No, Max, don't worry about it. See you tomorrow. Just come in when you are—free."

"Tony, I am not 'feeling better.' Don't you tell Trudy a goddam thing."

"Right Max. Between you and me. Just like old times."

"Tony, please."

"Talk to you tomorrow." The call ended.

"What a fucking mess," Max said as he put the phone down.

"Who was that?"

"My old partner," Max told her.

"What did he want?" Her eyes sparkled as she said the words.

"He wanted—to remind me of a meeting." He raised the ice pack, then set it back on his head, setting off a new wave of pain.

"Who's Trudy?" she asked.

"His wife. She..." Max let the words trail off. His stomach growled again, betraying his hunger.

"Oh!" she said, hearing it. "I forgot all about your dinner. Let me warm you something."

She leapt up from the couch, causing it to bounce slightly, and Max winced at the movement.

He watched her walk away.

Max had to admit she was attractive. He just found himself unable to act on it, or any other stirrings he felt from time to time.

Jenny was still out there, he knew it.

He looked at the ring on his left hand. It meant something to him, even if no one else understood. He took another deep swallow of the whiskey.

Kept sipping. He heard dishes clattering, what he assumed was a microwave running.

"Here you go," she said, returning.

Helen held a plate heaping with pasta covered in vegetables. He smelled seafood of some sort.

It smelled wonderful.

"Here," she said, setting up a small table in front of him, what they would have called a TV tray when he was a kid, but fancier.

"Thanks," he said. "It smells wonderful."

"Anytime, Max," she answered. As she sat, he noticed her top had come undone at the center, revealing the front clasp of a bra that matched the shirt.

His mind wandered to whether the bottoms might match too.

Snap out of it, Max.

He grabbed the glass, found it empty, and carefully put it back down.

"More?" Helen asked. She stood first, then bent over to get the glass, clearly intentionally providing him with a view.

"Sure," he said, feeling a bit dizzy. While she was gone, he dug into the food.

It tasted as good as it smelled, and he the plate was half empty by the time she returned, the glass half full of more Scotch.

Which he remembered was not his favorite brand, but he drank it anyway, wincing at the aftertaste of iodine.

She sat down next to him again, and watched him eat, and drink some more.

Max felt decidedly uncomfortable yet knew driving home was not an option. He needed a graceful way to turn Helen down for what she clearly wanted.

What he wanted in some ways as well.

He finished the plate, and watched Helen seductively remove it.

Her hips swayed their way toward the kitchen.

Max drained the whiskey glass. Looked at it.

His head spun. It ached, and he was dizzy.

Maybe I should get checked for a concussion, he thought. But he didn't feel that bad. Just tired.

"I think you should stay here tonight," Helen said. "You're in no shape to drive."

"I think so too," he said. Max felt like he might fall asleep any second. Yet he was strangely aroused. He needed to hide that, keep it to himself, so to speak.

"I have a spare room, if that's what you want," she purred, clearly making an offer, or rather solidifying the one she'd already made earlier, by her actions.

Her clothes, the candles, and the scent of her perfume.

"The spare room would be great," he heard himself say.

"Come on," she said. "If I don't get you to bed, you'll end up sleeping right there."

Max left the ice on the table. His head still throbbed, but it was better.

He didn't know if that was due to food, whiskey, or both.

Maybe the ice had even helped.

His eyelids were heavy.

Helen's touch was soft, her hands smooth against his skin as she took his arm.

He felt himself led him to a bedroom, where she left him standing in the middle of the floor as she drew back the covers.

He allowed her to sit him down, then kneel to remove his shoes, again offering the view down her blouse.

The scent of her hair filled his nostrils.

She pushed him back, and he winced as his head hit the pillow, then turned on his left side, away from his wounds.

Closing his eyes, he felt blankets pulled up around him.

Then fell into a deep, comfortable sleep.

Chapter Seventeen

Max woke to sunlight coming in at the wrong angle for the sun entering his apartment.

The bed was softer too.

Softer?

He threw back the floral comforter and placed his bare feet on the floor.

Bare feet? Floral comforter?

Helen had removed his shoes the night before, but his socks?

Max rubbed his hand over his bare chest, looking down. His belly was getting slack, not the six pack he'd always prided himself on. He should get back to the gym, right after...

Bare chest. Stood to stretch, clad only in boxers.

Shit.

He was in Helen's house, a spare bedroom? He hoped so. Had he undressed last night?

He couldn't remember doing so, and hadn't been so groggy he would not have noticed...

Max took a quick survey of the room. Dresser, clean. Chair, empty.

A second door, besides the one leading into the hallway, stood partially closed. Inside he could see what he assumed to be vanity lights and a mirror. A bathroom.

But no clothes were discarded anywhere.

And since Jenny was gone, Max had definitely turned into a discarder, seldom folding clothes except on laundry days.

Kept the math simple. Dirty clothes on the floor, clean ones in drawers or hung up.

Maybe Helen had picked them up and put them somewhere for him, maybe in the bathroom.

He needed to use that room anyway.

Making his way across the floor, arms folded across his chest, he opened the door and entered the unfamiliar room, managing to stub his toe on the door jamb on the way through.

"Ouch! Fuck!"

He did a dance to keep himself quiet, hoping Helen had not heard.

His clothes weren't in here either. But he took advantage of the location, closed the door, and relieved himself.

Turned to leave and saw the note on the counter.

Next to the sink, propped up against toothpaste and a nearly full bottle of mouthwash was a piece of paper, and a new toothbrush in the package.

The paper was folded, like a tent, and on the part facing him was his name: Max. In all four corners, a heart had been drawn.

Slightly frightened, he opened it up. Inside were the words:

"Robe is on the back of the door. Your clothes *yuck* are in the wash. Take your time getting ready."

Below the message was written Helen, with 'xo' marks on both sides.

Damn, what had he done?

A soft knock came on the bathroom door.

"Max, is that you?"

Silly question, he thought.

"Yes," he answered, not knowing what else to say.

"Your clothes are in the dryer, except for..." she stopped. He looked down at himself, then grabbed the robe and put it on, like she could see through the door.

He had to stop reacting like this.

"Good, good," he answered.

"Coffee is on. Come on out as soon as you're ready."

He heard, or imagined, retreating footsteps.

Max brushed his teeth, cinched up the robe the best he could, and went out to face reality.

He hoped he would have a break in the case today, even if it meant someone shooting at him.

That's something he could face more easily than this.

***

Helen's dog lay just outside the kitchen, looking hopefully at the both of them, as if they might throw her scraps at any moment.

The conversation topic, and having the dog nearby made Max uncomfortable on a couple of levels.

First, he found himself attracted to Helen. Not in just a sexual sense, but as a practical, funny woman. Just the attraction made him feel guilty.

Second, he didn't want to talk about Jenny and Samantha with a woman he was attracted to, but especially not about whether he'd worn a robe, what Jenny had slept in, and what having kids around had changed about that.

He didn't like talking about the past, because when he did, he was tempted to talk about Jenny as if she were a part of it, rather than the present.

And with her dog so close, he missed Houston too. It sounded so strange, in context with a missing wife and child, but it was true.

It all brought memories to the fore, and he did not like to remember, at least not when he wasn't alone, in his house or his apartment, with a bottle.

Jenny was missing, his daughter was dead. Simple as that.

He would find her and had to before he could really move on.

Still, it had been a long time.

So, when his phone rang, he scrambled to retrieve it from the pocket of the robe he was wearing.

"Max, I have something."

"What is it?" he asked Dr. Gamble.

"A few hits from the national database, and maybe an idea."

"Okay, give me about 40 minutes."

"Coffee?"

"No need. I am finishing up breakfast now."

"Up early?"

"Yes, I stayed..." he stopped.

"Stayed where?" she asked.

"Helen's place. I'll explain later."

"Bring her along. And Jennifer."

"Who?" Max asked.

"Her dog."

"Sure thing," Max said, and hung up.

"Dr. Gamble?" Helen asked.

"Yes," Max replied. "We're headed to her place after we finish eating. And we're supposed to bring your dog."

The dryer buzzed. An uncomfortable look crossed Helen's features. "I'll get your clothes. They should be done by now."

Max sopped up the last of his eggs with his toast and wondered what Dr. Gamble would have for them.

***

The numbers on the screen made his head ache.

Max wondered why vets and medical professionals couldn't use something Windows or Mac based that looked a little more modern.

Blueish-white letters on a dark background reminded him of high school, and programming in BASIC. The only way it would be worse would be if they were green on a greenish-black background.

Max's first computer had been a Silver Fox, an off-brand PC with a gigantic monochrome monitor. Now he had a very modern desktop in his office, fast, but one he used mostly to process photos.

To process photos.

Something clicked in his head.

He needed to take more pictures.

The dogs, the women, both had been a distraction. One of the ways Max had risen to the top of the detective ranks, and the reason he did so well as a P.I. was his shutterbug fetish. He often took dozens of photos at a particular scene, either with his phone, or a mirror-less DSLR, a camera halfway between a point and shoot and a true professional one.

The pictures themselves were not amazing, but the contents always revealed something.

One file on his desktop held 4,138 photos of his home in Queen Anne, both inside and out.

He had pictures of the dogs in this case, offered by the owners.

Pictures of the crime scene at the park.

But Max had neglected one thing: pictures of the owners.

The data on the screen reminded him he needed those photos.

Dog names were common and seemed to be like names for children. Every year, a list was published of the top 100, and inevitably it would contain some that seemed truly unique. Except to be on the list of the top 100, they were anything but.

The unique thing about each dog in the database was the name of the owner.

And the thing every owner on this particular list was they had traveled to a clinic to have an organ transplant for their dog.

There were only two centers listed that did transplants for dogs. One was in Maine. The other was listed right here, in Seattle.

And there were only two organ types available, liver and kidneys, or so it seemed at first glance.

He rubbed his eyes. He needed a team, to travel all over, contact these owners, but he didn't have one.

And he needed to go to the clinic here, but there was a problem. The only contact information was an e-mail address.

The clinic in Maine was different. It had a website, with an FAQ section, a contact form, an e-mail address, P.O. Box, and most importantly, a phone number. They advertised transplants for cats, and new, experimental canine transplants.

"What kind of clinic wouldn't have any contact information on the internet?"

"One that didn't want to be found," Dr. Gamble said over his shoulder.

"Why would that be?"

"Licensing. Illegal practice. Something."

"Then why would pet owners go there?"

"Desperation. There appear to be only two options. If the one in Maine is very busy, which I imagine they are, and is on the other coast, there could be a high demand not being met."

"Why does this site," he pointed to the screen, "say transplants are experimental for dogs?"

"It's harder to suppress the immune system of a dog. Transplants are often rejected, unless you can find a dog that is related. That is often difficult, especially in the world of mutts. In the world of breeders, it's unlikely an owner would risk the life of one dog for another."

"Do they have a breakthrough, a new method, or something?"

"Possibly. Why don't you call them and ask?"

"I think I will. Meanwhile, is there a way to organize the names of the owners who have sent their pets here for transplants, put them in a separate spreadsheet or something?"

"What are you thinking?"

"Some good old-fashioned leg work. Make some calls. Hopefully I won't have to call them all before I get an answer."

"I have patients to see. But I will get my receptionist to work on this between calls."

"Sounds good, thanks. Tell Helen she can go on home. I'll call her later."

"I just bet you will," Dr. Gamble said with a wink.

Max ignored her and opened the dialer on his phone, punching in the number to the clinic in Maine.

HARVESTED

Chapter Eighteen

"Canine Transplants, how can I help you?"

Max had been on hold for several minutes, and the voice startled him.

A masculine voice had initially answered, and he'd been directed to the correct department. The clinic's hold music was frequently interrupted by messages telling him the answers to his questions might be found on their website on the frequently asked questions page and thanking him for his patience.

The voice that finally answered was soft, feminine, and kind sounding.

"Hi there," he said. "My name is Max Boucher, and I'm a detective in Seattle." No need to cloud things with the facts: like that he was an ex-police detective, and now a private detective.

"What can I do for you Mr. Boucher?"

"I see you do canine liver and kidney transplants. I have some questions about your clients."

"We can't tell you anything about specific clients without a warrant, you understand," the voice turned cold.

"No, ma'am, nothing like that. I have more general questions."

"Perhaps I should get you the director of the program."

"If you think that would be the most helpful," Max answered, "that would be fine."

"I do," the voice said.

The hold music started again, followed by two rings, then silence.

Max looked at the phone to make sure it was still active and waited. After two minutes, he put the phone on speaker, and set it down on the desk.

He looked again at the computer, changing to the window that had held the database results.

The list was longer than he expected but could have been worse.

The names were split, with about six of ten under the Seattle clinic. Most of the patient dogs were older, but seven years was the oldest he found with a quick glance.

He needed this in another format. Simpler to search and cross-reference.

"Director Atwill," a voice said.

"Max Boucher," he answered, picking up the phone and turning off the speaker.

"I understand you are a detective with a question about some of our clients."

"I am," Max answered, almost clarifying, but thinking better of it.

Let the director think whatever he wanted.

"What exactly do you want to know? If you are investigating a failed procedure, I'm afraid—"

"Not that at all. I just need some education, more than likely."

"Okay. I'll answer what I can."

"You do dog and cat transplants but list the dog's as experimental."

"They are. The method we use is not yet approved. It is difficult to suppress a dog's immune system and achieve a successful transplant."

"So, I have been told."

"A team of our doctors determined difficult and impossible were two different things and developed a system that's 85% successful."

"The people who come to you are desperate and have nowhere else to turn."

"Of course. We are the only clinic of our kind in the nation."

"The only one?" Max asked. He wasn't yet ready to reveal his entire hand.

"Yes. The method is tricky, and complicated. Because it is experimental, it has to be done in a research lab, which we have here."

"What do you charge?"

"We cannot, per se. But the surgery center for dogs is a separate non-profit, and we encourage those who bring their pets to us to donate generously so the research can go on, and we can get canine transplants perfected and approved."

"And do they? Donate?" Max asked.

"Almost without exception," Director Atwill answered.

"Where do you get the donor organs?"

"We adopt animals from shelters and find homes for them after the transplants. We also breed some puppies here for the purpose and find homes for them as well. Often the owners who come to us for transplants also adopt the donor animal."

"Do you ever ship animals to other clinics?"

"Cats, yes. But there are no other dog clinics."

Max saw his chance and took it.

"What about the clinic in Seattle?"

"Clinic in Seattle?" the director asked.

Max wished he could see the other man. Study his face. But the suspicious voice that had warmed with his early questions went suddenly cold.

"Yes. There is a clinic here that does the same kind of canine transplants you do."

"I have heard. But they are not licensed."

"I see."

"Do you, Mr. Boucher? I don't think you do."

"Enlighten me."

"It is impossible for them to duplicate our techniques. We started from the ground up. Using an entirely new approach."

"No way at all?"

"No legitimate way."

"How about illegitimate?"

"I think our talk is over, Mr. Boucher. Good day."

The line went dead.

Just as Dr. Gamble walked into the room.

"Have you seen Helen?" she asked.

"No. I thought she was with you."

"When I went out front, the receptionist told me she'd stepped out. I got busy with other patients, and by the time I asked again, she still hadn't come back. I was hoping she said something to you."

"Nothing," Max said. "But I'll go look for her. I'll be back."

"What did you find out from the other clinic?"

"Nothing, but I suspect something. Once I find Helen, I'll need to make some more calls."

Dr. Gamble approached and hugged him, her head barely reaching his chin.

"Thanks Max," she said.

"You're welcome," Max said, wishing he'd never let her hug him the first time.

***

Max walked calmly out the front door, and then broke into a run, until he got to the Buick.

Helen was nowhere near the Skylark, and they had ridden together.

How long had she been gone?

Hell, it could be ten minutes or half an hour.

Across the street from the car, a homeless man leaned against a wall, facing him.

Veteran, Please Help, his sign read.

From his angle, he would be able to see the entrance to the clinic and the car, if he'd been watching.

Nothing else really mattered. Sober, high, nothing. This wasn't a police investigation, he simply wanted a direction.

He hurried over, digging out his wallet.

"Hey there," he said.

The man looked up at him. "What?"

Max held out a twenty. "Maybe you can help me for this?"

"Depends," the bum said. "I ain't into no sick shit."

"Me either," Max said. "Just wondering if you saw someone."

"Is it worth more to you if I did, or if I didn't?"

"Neither. I just want to know the truth."

The vagrant's eyes were clear. Not drunk, not high, just down on his luck.

Still, Max's instincts were pretty good, and he trusted them.

"Who you looking for?"

"A blond woman, tall, with a mutt."

"Sounds like a lot of people who came out of the vet's office."

"You're right."

"Although there was a woman who came out about twenty minutes ago or so who looked at the car you were just looking at, and then got in a cab that pulled up," the man asked.

"A cab pulled up?"

"Not typical in this neighborhood. My bet would be she called it."

"Interesting. You seem to know this area well."

"I lived here. Before..."

"Can you do me a favor?"

"You ain't paid me for the first one."

Max looked at the bill pinched in his fingers and handed it over.

"Thanks," the man said, stuffing the money deep into a pocket on the flannel shirt he wore.

"Can you watch that vet clinic? I'll give you a pad and pen. Can you write down who comes in and out, and the time?"

"I ain't got a watch," the bum said.

Max looked at the cheap Casio he wore on his wrist, one he seldom looked at now that he carried a phone everywhere.

"Here, take this one," he said, handing it over."

"For how long?"

"Until I get back."

"How long will that be?"

"Don't know," Max said. He pulled another two twenties from his pocket and held them out. "Will this do as a down payment?"

"Sure," the man said.

"Be right back," Max told him. He rushed across the street, entering Dr. Gamble's office.

The vet came out of the back office at the same time.

"Did you find her?" she asked.

"She's gone. Took a cab somewhere."

"How do you know?" she asked.

"Someone saw her," Max said, deciding to keep his new informant his secret for now.

"What are you going to do?"

"Find her. Tell your receptionist to keep working. I'll be back in a few hours, I hope."

"Be careful, Max."

"I will."

Max grabbed a yellow legal pad and a pen from the front desk. "I need these," he said.

Before the doctor or the red head manning the desk could ask why, he ran out the door, and across the street.

He practically threw the pad and the two twenties to the bum, and said, "Thanks for this."

Max ran back across the street, fired up the Skylark, and shifted into gear.

Shit, he still needed to get gas.

The timing was really shitty, but he sped up the block in the direction he knew there was a gas station, the opposite direction the cab had gone.

***

He squealed into the driveway and pulled up to the nearest open pump.

Card machine down. Cash only. ATM inside, a sign on the side of the pumps read.

He'd surrendered the last of his cash to the vagrant across from the clinic.

Max sprinted for the door but slowed to a walk inside. He didn't want to appear suspicious.

"ATM?" he asked the clerk.

"Back corner. Sorry about that." The clerk smiled, and Max thought he looked familiar, but could not place him.

He slid his card in and out of the slot and punched in his PIN. Drew out $60. Forty for gas, the other twenty for his pocket. Just in case.

In case of what, Max had no idea.

He hurried back up to the front, holding out two of the bills. "Forty on two," he said.

The clerk took them and fixed the sale.

"Thanks," he said, offering Max a receipt.

Max waved it away and started to leave.

Across the street stood Helen, her dog by her side.

"Helen?" he questioned aloud.

Max opened the door and rushed to the Skylark.

"Wait!" the cashier told him.

"What?" Max said, turning.

"You dropped this." The clerk held a twenty-dollar bill out.

Max ran back to get it, then turned back to look.

Helen was gone, if she had even been there at all.

"Thanks," he said over his shoulder, pocketing the bill.

"Have a nice day," the clerk said.

Max went out, and put the gas in the car, but some of his urgency had vanished. He needed to think this through a bit.

When he reached into his pocket to get his keys, he found there were two pieces of paper there. He pulled them out.

Two twenties.

He looked into the store, intending to go in and tell the clerk of his error, but the man who'd waited on him was gone, replaced by a younger man, clearly just old enough for the job, with the beginnings of a mustache, wearing a hat on backwards.

What the hell was going on here?

Chapter Nineteen

Instead of heading for Helen's, Max headed back to Dr. Gamble's clinic.

The parking spot he'd used before was taken. In fact, the street had become incredibly crowded, so he went around the corner and parked the Skylark between a large truck and one of the new ultra-small compact cars. Making sure it was locked, he walked toward the clinic.

The bum who had been across the street was gone.

There was no blanket, no evidence he'd been there at all.

Opening the door, he found the vet's lobby full of people.

Several of the dogs had bandages on their abdomens, or gauze wrapped around their mid sections.

In the ten minutes he'd been gone the waiting room had filled up.

"Max, over here!" he heard a voice call.

As he made his way through the crowd, several dogs sniffed at him, and several owners recognized him.

Eight, if he counted correctly.

There were a few owners sitting in the chairs at the edge of the room, but there were only about half a dozen seats.

One man with a cat carrier looked particularly distressed. A hissing came from inside the crate at his feet.

The receptionist greeted him. "Thank God, Mr. Boucher."

"What the hell is going on here?"

"They started to show up about a minute after you left. Several of the dog owners you were working with, several others whose pets have been missing, but did not report them to us or the police."

"They are all bandaged the same way Jeffrey was?"

"So far, the few the doctor has been able to examine have the same bandages, the same wounds. Surgical scars, professionally sewn up."

"The organ transplants," he said.

"More thorough tests will be needed, but it appears they all are down to one kidney."

"All of them?"

"As far as we can tell, every last one."

"Okay. Do you have the list you were working on before, the list for the Seattle clinic?"

"I'm not done. But I have a start."

"Give me what you have so far."

"Sure thing."

"What's taking so long?" a man asked from behind Max.

"The doctor is seeing every patient as fast as she can," the receptionist answered.

Max turned to face the man.

"Mr. Boucher!" the man said. "I don't know how you did it, or even what you did, but I'm glad our dogs are back."

"I—" Max started, but then simply said, "Thanks."

The man shook his hand, and a few others followed him. Max recognized them as the owners of the dogs missing from the park in Queen Anne. But it wasn't all of them.

And there were more dogs missing, he knew.

This was a ploy of some sort.

He took out his phone, and while Dr. Gamble's assistant transferred the file she had assembled so far to a thumb drive, he snapped pictures of everyone in the room as unobtrusively as he could.

No one seemed to take notice, or if they did, didn't care.

"Here you go, Mr. Boucher." The receptionist handed him the small device.

Just then, Dr. Gamble emerged from the patient rooms at the back of the office. She looked harried, her hair a mess.

"Max, thank God," the shorter woman said. "Can we talk for a minute?"

"Sure," he said, and followed her to the back. As they headed into the door, two owners with their dogs headed for the lobby.

"Make a follow up in the next two weeks or so, and we'll make sure your pets are doing okay," Dr. Gamble said, then turned to Max after they left.

"Good for business, huh?" he joked, and regretted it immediately.

"Sure," she said, running her fingers through her hair. "This is insane Max."

"I see that."

"No, you don't understand. All of the young, healthy dogs out there now have one kidney. So far the two I have seen were in very different stages of healing. One a couple weeks post op, almost healed entirely. The second only a few days out but recovering well."

"Both the same wound?"

"Not wound, Max. Incision. Professional. Well done."

"Okay, incision. Why now?"

"All I can think of is you."

"Me?"

"You are the first one looking at this, right? Who knows you suspect organ donation?"

"Helen, and the clinic in Maine, you and your staff."

"That's it?"

"That's all so far. I was going to call some friends at the department."

"So, someone tipped them off that you were close?"

"Impossible. I have not suspected the organ transplants that long. Releasing all these dogs took time to set up."

"Any theory as to why?"

"I don't have one yet."

"What's next?"

"I'm headed back to my office and my apartment. I haven't been there in a couple of days. Maybe I can put some of this together."

"Okay. Call me tonight?"

"Will do," Max said. The vet hugged him again, and he walked out. He turned back and watched the lobby full of people and pets as she called the next one back to be examined.

He told her he had no theories. He'd lied again, but like the other lies he'd told so far in this case, he thought it was for good reason.

***

The air smelled stale. He opened a window, even though it was cold and misty, but just a crack.

In his apartment, he changed into a clean shirt and jeans. Looked around the room and realized he needed to do some laundry, seriously.

Later.

He went downstairs to his office. Fired up his desktop. It took a while to boot up, as the screen informed him updates were being installed.

At the same time, he accessed his phone and made sure the pictures he had taken at the vet were uploaded to the cloud.

The transfer from phone to online storage was complete.

His home screen loaded quickly, he plugged the thumb drive into a USB hub on his desk and opened the file.

Max scanned the list of names. None of those visible were familiar.

Not knowing for sure why, he opened the pictures he had taken at the vet and scanned the faces. The ones he recognized were from Queen Anne, nothing unexpected.

He also looked at the dogs but saw nothing unusual beyond the similar bandages they all wore.

On a whim, he decided to try something. He opened his browser and Googled "vet offices near my location."

Several came up, and he dialed the first one.

The phone rang several times. Finally, a stressed sounding voice answered. "Bay Area Canine Clinic, how many I help you?"

"This is Detective Max Boucher," he said. The half-truth was getting easier to say every time he used it.

"What can I do for you, Detective? Is your pet an existing patient?"

"I don't have a pet at the moment. I have—"

"We're very busy today. What can I do for you?"

"Are you very busy because several previously missing dogs showed up at your clinic with their owners, all with bandages covering surgical scars or incisions?"

"Yes, how did you know?"

"Thanks for your help," he said, and hung up.

The next three clinics he reached were experiencing a similar influx of patients, some to a lesser degree than others. He looked over the pictures from the vet again, counting. A little over a dozen dogs. Not really a huge number, but the small size of the waiting room had made them seem overwhelming.

From initial impressions it seemed maybe a hundred dogs had returned to clinics all over, at nearly the same time, or at least on the same day.

Another thing to check.

On a whim, he called Seattle animal control.

The phone rang several times, and then went to a voice mail box.

Max left his name and number.

It seemed they were very busy as well.

Something nagged at the back of his head.

Helen had run out. Disappeared. He thought he had spotted her down the street, but she had disappeared before he could verify it.

Max dialed her number.

It rang several times. No answer, no voice mail.

He had a second number for her. Cell? Home? He had labeled them both mobile, the default in his phone contacts. The call also yielded no results.

Looked up to see his screen saver running. A slide show of Jenny and Samantha, many of the pictures showing his girls with his dog, Houston.

Max slid his mouse to wake up the computer as one last one of Jenny and Houston standing next to Bridal Falls in Yosemite crossed the screen.

A lump rose in his throat, for both of them as he studied the spreadsheet again.

Owner names, dog names, addresses.

All of them had come here, to Seattle, looking for hope for their sick animals.

Were they wrong? Would he have done the same thing?

Maybe not. Maybe he wouldn't have resorted to illegal means. But to save his daughter, save his wife? You bet he would have.

Maybe even for Houston, if he could be sure no one was getting hurt.

The dogs were back. Maybe not all of them, but several. This time released in a large group.

But what if before they had been released one at a time, spaced apart? How often were the stories of a dog that disappeared, and then returned, maybe with some scars, but alive?

How often did families rejoice, but never release details to anyone? How often were those scars surgical, but vets never reported it? Who would they report it to?

Sure, maybe there were illegal surgeries being performed on dogs. But if both dogs, the donor and recipient, made it most of the time, if neither were hurt...

In this case, sometimes sick dogs were taken, and then returned. Some had diagnoses with them, ones that might have otherwise passed the owner's notice.

Who were the victims? Owners who missed their dogs for a short time?

The donor dogs, whose long-term health might or might not be affected?

Certainly not the recipients of the organs, even if their owners paid a little extra for surgeries.

And who benefited? Those same owners, and those who ran the clinic. The ones who got paid.

Follow the money, he'd learned long ago.

He looked at the spreadsheet again. He could see the first thirty or so records, some dating back five years.

He scrolled down and stopped.

Number three in the 'E' section.

Owner name: Ebbley, Helen.

Dog name: Ricky.

City: Seattle.

The address listed was hers in Queen Anne, to be exact.

Ricky, not Jennifer. A male dog.

Max highlighted the record, and scanned across to the last two columns, outcome, and notes.

Unsuccessful Transplant, the outcome said.

Patient rejected the donor organ, the notes said. Time elapsed following surgery, three days. Owner informed.

He scanned back across. The date of the surgery was three months ago.

Max wondered what else he might not know about Miss Helen Ebbley.

Closing the spreadsheet, he pulled up another window, and opened a background check program he paid monthly for and typed in all the information he knew about her.

A short list came up.

Her current address, the same for the last three years.

Birth date. Helen was 46, very close to his guess at her age.

Credit score, not bad. No overdue or outstanding debts. Appeared to own her house outright.

Purchased three years ago, apparently with cash.

Before that, nothing.

He looked closer.

The earliest date for any of her records was a little over three years ago. The day after Jenny disappeared.

He scrolled down. There was one other thing.

Her title.

Dr. Helen Ebbley, Veterinary Medicine.

Yet her records didn't reveal a job ever. Helen Ebbley was a ghost, and a vet. Passing off a dog that wasn't hers as hers.

Suddenly finding her, finding the clinic in Seattle seemed very important.

Max opened another browser window and dialed a friend of his at the police department.

As he was about to hit send, his phone rang.

Above the number on the screen, a name appeared.

Helen.

Part Three: Found

"The pen will never be able to move fast enough to write down every word discovered in the space of memory. Some things have been lost forever, other things will perhaps be remembered again, and still other things have been lost and found and lost again. There is no way to be sure of any this."

--Paul Auster

HARVESTED

Chapter Twenty

"Hello, Helen," Max answered.

"Hi Max," she said.

"I think we need to talk," he said, keeping his voice level.

"I can explain," she said.

"Good. I could use that. Where can we meet?"

A long pause followed. Max resisted the temptation to fill the silence. Whoever started talking first, lost.

Finally, she sighed. "I'll call you back."

The call ended.

Max finished the call he'd been about to make.

"Randall," the voice at the other end of the line answered flatly.

"Randall, it's Boucher."

"Max, Jesus, it has been ages."

"Too long, I know. Listen, I need a favor."

"How big a favor?"

"I have a 25-year-old Laphroaig I'll share."

Randall whistled. "That is big. How much trouble am I going to get into for this?"

"None at all. I just need to find out something, fast."

"Hit me with it. I'm your man."

"Background on a Helen Ebbley."

"You are using the software I turned you on to, right?"

"Yeah, but that's where this one goes sideways. Miss Ebbley appeared three years ago. There's not a trace of her before that. I'd like to know who Helen Ebbley was before she became...well, who she is today."

"What do you have?"

"Almost nothing. Except her fingerprints must be on file somewhere, and her picture too. She's a doctor—well a vet."

"I'll start with the American Association of Veterinary State Boards and go from there. I am assuming she is licensed in Washington?"

"That's what the background check says, so I am assuming the same thing."

"All right Max. Thanks for a real challenge. I'll get back to you."

"Thanks Randall."

"And Max?"

"Yeah?"

"I'm going to hold you to that drink. It's been too long since we shared a dram."

"Damn right."

He ended the call and leaned back in his chair. Now what?

Now, he needed to find the location of the clinic in Seattle. The problem? The area was huge and diverse. The clinic could be anywhere.

Max took out a piece of paper and started to list the neighborhoods.

Beacon Hill, where he lived now. Not likely. Too much crime, and too many regular patrols and police raids. Someone would notice a bunch of dogs going in and out.

Queen Anne. Bainbridge. Ballard and Bellevue, Belltown, Capitol Hill.

He ran through the list in his head, then stopped.

If you were going to hide a dog surgery, how would you do it? In a normal vet's office, of course.

He clicked on his open browser and searched for vets in Seattle.

Over 1,000 results.

Great.

He sat back, and then opened a map of Seattle on his computer.

Began to scan around the screen.

C'mon Max. Where would you...

Edmonds. Mixed, industrial and residential. Near the waterfront. Relatively easy freeway access via 104 and close to the ferry.

He clicked on another tab. Refined the larger vet search to "near Edmunds, Seattle."

Five.

One on fifth, one on ninth, and a relatively new one.

Think Pawsitive Veterinary Surgery on Edmonds Way.

Cute name.

What are you basing this on Max? he asked himself.

"Nothing," he said aloud. "Nothing but instinct."

His phone rang again. It was Helen.

Or the woman who called herself Helen.

"Hey there," he answered.

"Did you figure it out yet?" she asked.

"Figure what out?"

"Where the clinic is."

"No." This time it wasn't a lie. Max suspected something but had no facts.

"How about we meet for dinner?" she asked. "Someplace public. Comfortable for both of us."

"Why do I think you already have someplace in mind?"

"You know Herfy's, on Edmonds?"

Max did but chose to lie. "No. I don't know that area at all."

"Liar," she answered. "See you there at six. Don't be late."

The call ended, and Max noted the time.

Quarter to five. It would take him 15 minutes in normal traffic, a little longer now.

He sat for a minute, looking at the map. Weighing the possibilities in his mind.

Then decided to get changed and leave early.

Max checked his smell, decided he could use a shower, but didn't have time.

He raced up to his apartment, slapped on some deodorant, and brushed his teeth.

Looking into the mirror, he ran his fingers through his hair, trying to make the short strands lay down rather than stick up at odd angles. Good enough.

Max raced down the stairs, and to the Skylark. Hopped in, fired it up, and squealed his tires as he pulled out of his space.

He looked back in his mirror, at the door to Shorty's, the street, still quiet, that would not wake until late in the evening.

Hoping to return in time for a drink, or seven, Max turned his attention to the road ahead, and the questions he hoped would be answered soon.

***

Max's phone rang as he stared at the building across the street. "Boucher," he answered.

"Max, it's Tony. Weren't you going to come in today?"

"Shit! I forgot."

"Randall fessed up. Said he is checking some shit for you."

"He is."

"Can you do me a favor?"

"Tony, for you, anything."

"Keep me better updated, would you?"

"I'll try." He hung up.

The clinic sat right on the sidewalk next to what appeared to be an apartment house.

The building itself was three stories. The lower level seemed to hold the vet's office, or what he was starting to think of as the front for whatever was going on, while above it there were windows with curtains, similar to his apartment over his office in Beacon Hill, with the exception these buildings appeared to be much nicer.

An awning extended over the sidewalk, and a small sign under it said simply, "Think Pawsitive."

Max drove by, debated about going in.

Except he didn't have a dog with him.

It was right around the corner from the burger place where he was meeting Helen, and he had about twenty minutes.

Circling the block, he noticed a space opened up with a line of sight to the clinic, so he pulled the Buick in, and watched.

No one went in or out. The place looked oddly quiet.

Max could not tell from the front but knew this neighborhood. The buildings were not large.

By his count, dozens, if not over one hundred dogs had been released on the Seattle area in the last 12 hours.

Whatever else this place was, there was no way a hundred dogs were stored here without someone noticing.

Of course, there were other empty businesses on the street. An empty garage he'd noticed around the corner. One he thought might have been empty for years.

Then again, maybe he was wrong.

Maybe this was just a normal vet's office, and nothing more than routine checkups, dental cleanings, and vaccinations took place here.

The longer he watched, the more suspicious he became, and for no logical reason because nothing happened.

Which could mean nothing or everything.

He wasn't close enough to see if the open sign was lit.

Max decided to leave the Skylark parked right where it was and do a walk by on the way to the restaurant.

He was about to get out, when the door to the clinic opened.

Helen walked out, and turned toward Edmonds, and the restaurant where they were supposed to meet.

Max slipped out of the Buick and stepped on to the sidewalk on the opposite side of the street.

He slowed opposite the vet office, and read a sign on the door that said, clearly:

Closed Until Further Notice.

The front windows were covered with dark cloth of some kind, maybe blue, almost black.

As he stood studying the place, he swore they moved, as if someone had been watching him. Another moment of staring at nothing happening again, Max kept walking down to the corner.

Ahead, he saw Helen turn and walk into the restaurant, so he followed.

As he walked through the door, she spotted him, and waved, as if they were the best of friends.

Max walked over to the table and sat down opposite her.

His phone buzzed in his pocket, and he took it out, glancing at the screen.

It was Randall. Damn, he would have to call him back. He couldn't talk freely in front of the subject he was checking on.

He tapped the screen to ignore.

Two seconds later, his phone buzzed again. A text, from a number he didn't know.

But it was 206. Had to be Seattle.

Max tapped the app to open the message, while across from him, Helen grinned and watched.

The text was simple.

"It's Randall," it said. "9-1-1. Text me."

Slowly, Max placed the phone back in his pocket, thinking soon he would have to come up with a reason to go to the bathroom, or excuse himself some other way.

Helen smiled. "Not good news?" she said.

"I don't know yet," Max said. "Why don't we start with you telling me your real name?"

"Let's order first," she answered, and just as she said the words, a waitress approached.

Max looked down at the menu, completely unsure of what he wanted.

Suddenly, he wasn't hungry at all.

HARVESTED

Chapter Twenty-One

"Helen" remained silent.

Max did the same.

Their burgers came. Max ordered a coke rather than a beer. Sipped it, and found it much too sweet for his taste, just as he remembered from the last time he'd had one.

Where they were sitting did not suit him at all. He couldn't see the front door, or most of the restaurant behind him. He felt exposed.

He found himself looking right and left, even checking the mirror over the counter, the convex one the employees used to keep an eye on the diners.

Probably there was a camera behind it. He hoped so.

Yet there was no solid reason for his paranoia.

No threats came, and the longer they did not come, the more nervous he became.

"You've hardly touched your burger," Helen said.

"I'm not that hungry."

"That's not like you Max."

He slammed his hand on to the table, and she jumped. For a moment, the noise of others dining around them stopped, and a few people openly stared.

Max stared back, until they looked away and the chatter resumed.

"Let's cut the shit, Helen, or whatever the fuck your name is. I want to know the truth. Where are the rest of the dogs? What the hell is going on?"

"We're on the same side Max."

"Somehow I find that hard to believe."

"Why?"

"Everything you've told me was a lie. You're a vet. You seem not to have existed before three years ago. You are not who you say you are. This morning, you disappear, and suddenly several dogs are released on the city."

"What could I have to do with that?"

"I don't know. But Jennifer is not your dog. Your dog was part of...whatever is going on here."

"How do you figure?"

"You are on a list. For a clinic in Seattle no one seems to know where is, and your dog's transplant was a failure."

"What does that even mean, Max?"

Max slammed his hand onto the table again. Helen's water glass jumped, and she barely caught it before it fell over.

A few more patrons stared, but he did not care this time.

"I don't know!" he yelled. "But you are connected to whatever is going on, and I want to know how!"

"Let me ask you a question, Max," she said calmly.

"Is everything okay here?" A man appeared at their table, skinny, nervous, and young, but wearing a name tag that read "manager."

"Fine. Just fine," Max said.

"Ma'am?"

"It's okay," Helen said.

"Please keep it down," he said. "You're disturbing the other customers."

"We will," Max said. "Sorry, it won't happen again."

Helen waited until the man was out of earshot.

"Why did I hire you then, Max?"

He felt his face redden but controlled himself. Barely.

"I wish I knew," he hissed. "Why don't you tell me?"

"It might be easier to show you," she said.

"I'm not going with you anywhere," he told her.

"Are you sure?"

"Not until you tell me your real name."

"Helen" sighed and picked up her purse from the seat next to her.

She pulled out a wallet and took out a business card. She turned it over and wrote on the back.

Max watched, waiting, breathing deeply to diffuse his temper.

From another pocket in the bag, she took a folded piece of newspaper.

She looked right and left, as if to make sure no one was watching or approaching.

Sliding both over to him in a small pile, she kept her hand on top.

"Read. Then we go. Not a word here. Understand, Max?"

"I can't..."

She took her hand off the pile, and brushed the pen off the table, onto the floor.

"Oops. Can you be a dear and get that for me?" Her eyes darted down, and Max knew she had another motive, but keeping his eyes on her, leaned over to retrieve the pen.

As his head passed below the table, Max saw she had a small caliber pistol pointed at his waist.

"Not a word, Max," she said as he sat up.

"You wouldn't shoot me here."

"You might want to read first, before you jump to that conclusion."

Max put his fingers on the pile, and she motioned for him to go ahead.

He took the card first. "Martina Dudiki, DVM."

Flipped it over. Written there were the words, "This was me."

Max opened the news article, carefully.

Helen, or Martina, watched every move.

The headline made his heart stop.

"Family and Pets Slaughtered, Wife Disappears"

Underneath he read the first paragraph.

"Edward Dudiki, a local attorney, arrived at his home in Albuquerque to find his daughter dead at the dining room table, and his wife missing. The family dog was also killed, apparently protecting the family from the intruder. The police followed a trail of blood out the back door of the home but found nothing. The investigation is still ongoing, and the status of his wife, Martina, is still officially stated as missing, although an unnamed spokesman for the police stated they are not hopeful."

Max looked for a date, but the article had been cut from the main body of the paper. He looked up at her, felt his eyes water.

"When?" he asked hoarsely.

"Four years ago."

"Four years?" Max couldn't breathe.

His own Jenny had disappeared three years ago, the scenario nearly identical.

As had another woman in their neighborhood.

The other woman's body had been found, in the waterfront district. She'd been murdered.

Jenny's body was never recovered, but the police assumed she was dead.

Max knew differently. She was alive. He had no doubt.

Martina's hand appeared over the table. She must have put the gun away.

From her purse, she pulled another article. Max could see the sadness in her face as she handed it over.

He unfolded it carefully.

"Prominent Local Attorney Commits Suicide."

He looked up at her, but she was looking away. Maybe at the mirror above the counter. Maybe nowhere at all.

"Edward Dudiki, whose wife remains missing, was found in his home on Friday when he didn't show up for work, and coworkers reported him missing. The cause of death was an apparent suicide. Mr. Dudiki was found in his vehicle, in the garage, with all of the doors closed. The deceased has no surviving children, but his brother expressed his sorrow.

"'Edward was a good man. He took the loss of his family very hard and has not been the same since. I can only hope he found peace in death he could no longer find in life.' Edward was 47 years old."

The article ended. Max set it on top of the others. Pushed the pile back toward her.

Helen took it, silently, and put it back in her purse.

Max took an awkward sip of soda but needed something for the lump in his throat. Something stronger.

"You want to come with me now?" she said. "I really do have something to show you."

"I want to know your story," he said.

"You will, Max. But not here."

She nodded toward the convex mirror. Near the front door, two wiry oriental men appeared to be also looking in the mirror. At them.

"Then let's go," Max said. "But no more games. You tell me the truth."

"Deal, Max," the woman said. She slid out of the booth, and he followed.

She brushed past the two men by the door, and Max did the same. He glanced back from time to time, but they did not appear to follow.

Quite possibly because they already knew where they were going.

***

As they walked, Max's phone buzzed in his pocket.

A text message.

Same number as earlier. Randall. "Are you okay? Call me."

He stopped. "Hang on a sec," he told Helen. She turned to wait, as he stepped under a streetlight so he could see better.

"With Helen. Okay. Know who she is," he texted.

Phone buzzed a moment later. "No, you don't."

A picture followed a second later. A mug shot, showing a younger Helen, facing forward and to the side, with numbers and her name on a placard.

He looked up at her.

"You okay?" she asked.

"Yeah, just fine," he lied. Again.

"You sure?" she said, gesturing at the phone.

"Just some interesting new information," he said, smiled, and slid the phone into his pocket. He checked the position of the .45 under his jacket, but nothing more.

Sure, he'd seen she was armed. But he'd be damned if he'd be intimidated.

Still, he turned up his instincts as they walked along.

Shortly after they rounded the corner, they came to the door he'd seen her come out.

"Clever name," he said.

"Thanks," she said, unlocking the door.

He glanced around before following her inside. He didn't see anyone behind them.

Helen disarmed the beeping alarm system. Flipped on some lights.

"Let me give you the tour," she said.

"No."

"No?" she turned. "You worked so hard to find this place, even figured it out on your own, or so you think, and you don't want a tour?"

"I want answers first."

She shook her head. "We'll talk while we walk."

"And if I say no?"

"Who do you think those men were in the restaurant, Max?"

"The Koreans? They are not Yong's men. I'm not sure who they are. Chijon family maybe"

"Ever hear the phrase, 'the enemy of my enemy is my friend'? "

"Of course."

"They are our real enemy Max. Both of us"

"Are you my enemy, Martina?"

She turned toward him slowly. "Don't call me that. My name is Helen. I haven't been Martina for a long time."

"Fine," he said. "Helen then. Are you my enemy?"

"I don't think so. We really are on the same side, Max."

"Then who or what the fuck are you?" he asked. He felt the anger rising again. Max was not one for hitting women, but he wanted to grab her, shake her, make her give him the answers.

"Easy, Max," she said. "You want to hear my story, walk with me."

Balling his fists, feeling his nails dig into his palms, he obeyed.

The lobby was like any other doctor's, or vet's office, he supposed. He'd only really been in Doctor Gamble's. Jenny had always handled Houston's doggy doctor visits.

The magazines were different. *Dog Fancy. Breeder's Monthly.* Things along that line.

A door led to the back offices, and as soon as she opened it, Helen stopped.

Max nearly ran into her, and then the smell hit him too. Blood.

"Something's wrong," she said.

"You mean something else?" Max said. "Seems to me there are quite a few things wrong here."

"It doesn't smell like this, usually."

At the end of the hall, something metallic clattered to a tile floor.

Max drew his pistol, clicked off the safety.

"Move," he commanded.

Five doors led off the hallway, he assumed to examination rooms.

Two were open all the way.

He could use a partner, some kind of backup.

But if he called the police, he might lose his chance at answers, not only about Martina/Helen, but Jenny.

Besides, it might be nothing.

The movies got it all wrong. When clearing a room, by yourself, you entered low, not high, limiting both visibility and making yourself a smaller target.

In a crouch, as low as he could go and remain on his feet, Max ducked around the first door jamb. The room was empty, at first glance. A large metal table stood in the center, and he was unable to see all the way around it.

He entered, still staying low and silent, and checked behind it.

Nothing. No one.

Left the room. Helen watched. Her face showed no fear.

He didn't take the time to wonder why.

Moving on to the next door, he strained to hear any sound at all.

Nothing.

The next door was closed. He left it that way. Anyone coming out of it would make noise, alert him, and he'd have time to react.

Besides the sound seemed to come from the room at the end of the hall.

Max slid along, the wall at his back, toward the final open door. Across from him was another one, closed.

"Imaging," the sign on the door said.

He spun low into the final room.

There was no one there, but it was far from empty.

A dog lay on the table, apparently mid-surgery. Its eyes were closed, but its sides rose and fell as it breathed.

Max could not tell the breed at first glance. Mainly because his vision was overwhelmed by the tubes in its nose, and the bag of what appeared to be blood hanging on an I.V. stand.

On another bed in the corner, another dog lay. It merely appeared to be sleeping. A bandage similar to those he'd seen earlier in the day was wrapped around its middle.

A screen overhead showed a close-up view of the wound in the dog on the main table. He put the safety on the .45 and pointed it at the floor.

"Jesus," Helen breathed from the doorway behind him. "Max, you have to help me finish."

"What?" he asked.

"You have to help me finish. If you don't, this dog will die."

"What is this? Who was here? Where did they go?"

"There's no time to explain, but I will, I promise. Only if you help me."

Max looked closer at the animal. It didn't look at all like Houston. But off to one side, on the counter opposite, he saw a collar with tags. Two.

These dogs belonged to someone.

What would you do if it was a person lying there Max?

I'd call an ambulance, he answered himself.

And if there wasn't one? Then I'd help.

So fucking do it.

The conversation in his brain was a short, quick one.

"Fine," he said, holstering the weapon. "What do I do?"

The odd thing was, the room did not smell like blood. It smelled like antiseptic and a hospital.

"Put on these gloves," she said, as she scrubbed her arms quickly in a sink to one side.

"Don't I need to scrub in or something?"

"No time to teach you. I shouldn't be doing it in here as it is."

"What do you mean?"

"Max! Shut up. We don't have time. Come over here. Quick lesson for you. Those are clamps, those are sutures, that is a scalpel. Got it?"

"I think so," he answered.

"You better."

Helen put on some glasses with lights on either side. She looked at the surgery site carefully for a minute, swinging a magnifying light over the area too.

"Damn," she whispered.

"What?" Max asked.

"Clamps," she answered.

Max handed them over.

For the next twenty minutes, he followed her instructions. She only yelled at him twice for screwing up.

Finally, she was bandaging up the dog's abdomen.

"Are we good?" he asked as she went about what appeared to be routine tasks for her.

"Probably," she said. "Too early to be sure. But he won't die today."

"Good," Max said. "Can I—" he pointed to the sink.

"Sure," she said.

"I still want some answers you know," he said as he scrubbed, his back to her. "It's admirable, what you just did, but—"

"Max," she said softly.

He stopped scrubbing and turned.

"Shut off the water," a voice said in a heavy accent.

Max turned to see a short, round oriental man. Next to him, a taller slim man held a pistol under Helen's chin.

"Shut off the water," he said again. Max turned and obeyed.

"Now you will come with us, Mr. Boucher. First, hand over your weapon."

Max slid the .45 from his shoulder holster and held it out.

"Now phone."

Max handed that over as well. The man took the back off, removed the battery, and threw both pieces into the trash.

Helen shook her head at him. Looked terrified.

Max simply smiled back at her and nodded.

The .38 in the holster on his ankle felt like it weighed a thousand pounds.

"Let's go," the man gestured for Max to go ahead of him. He turned around Max's .45 and pointed it at them. "No funny stuff, or you both get hurt."

'Hurt' sounded like 'hut.' Max hated the man right away.

Not for pointing his own gun at him, and certainly not for pointing it at Helen. He hated the man for taking away his chance at answers about Jenny.

Max intended to escape as soon as possible and take Helen with him.

Even if he had to kill these two men to do it.

.

.

Chapter Twenty-Two

They didn't search him. It was the one thing they overlooked.

For their oversight, Max was grateful.

But they did everything else textbook.

If the textbook was hostage taking or kidnapping, whatever you wanted to call their actions.

Every time he was not bound, they held a gun on Helen.

Under other circumstances, he might not even have cared. True, Helen had hired him, and he still wasn't sure why, but she'd also deceived him, and he'd fallen for it.

If it wasn't her clinic, she wanted him to find, even if it was her clinic at all, what had she wanted him to investigate, specifically?

It all tied back to the disappearance of the dogs.

These thoughts ran through his head as they were driven through the city in the back of a van. He tried to count the turns, figure distance and count lefts and rights, but the driver was either wise to the fact he might try something like that, or the route they needed to take was actually windy enough to defeat his sense of direction and distort the passage of time.

Helen sat across from him. They were on actual seats, and the van was not black.

It was a service van, the letters on the side Chinese, maybe.

Or Korean.

But there was no sign of Yong, nor did he recognize either of the men.

And the inside of the van was comfortable. The seats were set up like those in a limo, or at least Max assumed so.

He'd rarely been in a limo, in fact the last time might have been the night of his wedding, when he and Jenny had rented one to take them to the airport for the first leg of their honeymoon.

The men handcuffed him to a chain coming from a ring set into the carpeted floor.

Helen was similarly restrained.

He wanted to ask her questions, interrogate her.

Where were you for a year?

Who took you?

How did you get away?

A thought had formed, one he hated, yet that seemed so right he could not deny it.

Martina had reappeared as Helen three years ago, one day after Jenny disappeared.

He wondered if Jenny had been her replacement, whatever it was she had been doing.

Max did not want to imagine.

And then, if she'd been released, or maybe escaped after a year, then since Jenny had been missing for three...

Maybe she was out there somewhere. New identity. New name. New city, and new job.

But she would have reached out to him, wouldn't she?

Unless she couldn't.

The problem being, Max could imagine a hundred scenarios where that might be true. Because he'd been a cop. Now he did the same job, just for less money and private clients.

He also knew the odds. But he did not want to believe them.

Other people's wives were kidnapped. Raped. Killed. It couldn't happen to him.

She'd been taken, sure. But none of those other things had happened to Jenny. She was still alive, maybe even free.

He looked across at Helen. Formerly Martina. She was his proof, and she had answers.

He pulled at the chains in frustration.

Helen shook her head at him, before one of the men turned his weapon on Max.

"No funny business," was all he said.

The van stopped. Max heard noises outside.

Voices.

The sound of a helicopter, passing overhead.

Were they near the airport?

No, he hadn't heard any planes at all.

Then the van lurched forward a short distance, went over a bump, then rolled a little further.

It stopped.

The side door slid open, and Max was greeted with an odd sight,

What appeared to be a surgical table sat in front of what appeared to be a tarp, or some kind of temporary wall.

The floor was concrete.

The smell of disinfectant was very strong, like that of a hospital. Combined with a strong scent of salt. The blend of the two stung his nostrils.

The actual ceiling seemed to be very far over their heads.

What was the table being used for?

But Max didn't want to follow the path his mind laid out for him.

Because he already knew the answer.

***

A slim man Max recognized undid the lock holding the handcuffs to the chain but left the cuffs on. Another did the same with Helen.

The squat man, the one who appeared to be the leader of whatever this was, appeared at the side door.

"Get out," was all he said.

Max did as he was told, and Helen followed.

The air was cold. Damp. They had to be near the sound.

Which in Seattle, meant they could be anywhere. There was little else to indicate their location.

"Don't I recognize you?" Max asked the thin man.

"Yeah, you cost me twenty bucks. Otherwise, you might have had answers sooner."

He recognized the clerk from the store. The one who had suddenly disappeared after distracting him. After he thought he'd seen Helen.

"Martina," another voice said. Max turned his head that direction, and saw Helen, frozen, staring at a man standing in front of her. He looked vaguely familiar as well.

"What are you doing here?" she asked.

"The same as you, I suppose. Making money."

"But what is this? All of this?"

"You mean you don't know?"

It wasn't just his face. It was his voice. Max felt like he'd talked to him before. On the phone maybe?

"I used to believe in what you were doing," Helen said.

"It was a shame you disappeared." The man frowned, in what Max thought might be genuine sorrow.

It was the director. From the clinic in Maine. He'd suspected Helen. Suspected Yong even. And he'd been wrong.

"You needed a bigger, more reliable source for organ donors," Max interjected.

"As I told you on the phone Mr. Boucher, people are very generous in their donations. Almost desperate at times."

"To think I worked for you. Believed in what you did." Helen's face was red with anger.

"What's really happening here?" Max asked.

"I tried to help out on my own, Max. I really did mean well."

"I fear you were getting close to answers. Especially that one." It was Yong's voice from behind him.

Max turned. He saw Yong but cuffed in a similar manner to himself and Helen.

"You. But why...?"

"He used to be helpful. Until his daughter pricked his conscience. Then you came along and turned him into a liability."

"What do you mean by that?"

"Oh, he didn't tell you?" the man laughed.

"How about you refresh my memory?"

"He used to be one of our suppliers."

"Interesting."

"Do you wonder, Max, why I just didn't kill you, rather than bringing you here?"

"Every other turn in this case, I've been wrong. I don't suppose it'll be suddenly different now."

"You're a funny man, Mr. Boucher. I didn't think it of you before, but you're very amusing."

"Glad I could entertain you."

"Sit them down," the short man commanded.

Three chairs appeared. Max felt himself led to one and grimaced as the cuffs were attached to it roughly, securing his hands behind him.

Helen was next, and then Yong.

Max took a quick count of their opponents. The director, the clerk, and five others. Small, wiry men, but they all looked strong and athletic. They were probably selected for something other than their ability with animals.

Even if he got to the gun in his ankle holster, and was dead accurate with every shot, he'd still leave at least one man standing. He might be able to take out that one, if he were free.

Still, the odds were not good. By then he'd have lost the element of surprise.

"You still have not told me your name, or why we are here," Max said.

"And I probably won't," the man said. "But we will see, soon."

Max saw one of the men move toward Helen with a syringe. He wanted to warn her. But as he opened his mouth, he felt a stick in his arm as well.

Turning his head, he saw the same happening to Yong.

Just before the lights went out.

Chapter Twenty-Three

Max woke to the sound of dogs barking, several of them. Followed by a similar number of whimpers, and silence.

Max opened his eyes, but it did no good.

He couldn't see a thing.

The air was filled with the mixed smell of dog shit and dog food. A weaker, underlying odor he assumed was piss.

Max thought he preferred the bleach salt smell from before.

Before.

Before what?

Before here, he answered himself.

The room, with the surgical table.

"Helen?" he asked the darkness. A feminine moan answered, but that was all.

"Yong?" he asked.

"I am awake," he heard. "At least I think so."

"What is going on? Where are we?"

"You do not know?"

"No, I said—"

"I thought you were bluffing. This is bad, very bad."

"How would I know where we are, Yong?"

"You did not open envelope I gave you?" There was panic in that voice.

"Envelope?" Then Max thought back to the restaurant, and their conversation about Yong's daughter.

Two envelopes.

"This one is for you," Yong had told him.

Where were they?

He'd been knocked out and woken up in his Skylark. Again.

Then had gone to Helen's, and the day's events had followed, much too quickly.

He'd forgotten all about both the envelopes and Yong's daughter.

"I thought you'd look at it right away," Yong's voice chided him.

"I...well, it's complicated."

"You shared that envelope with no one?"

"No one."

"Not your police friend?"

"I don't even know for sure where it is. Maybe my car. If you hadn't hit me on the head so hard, maybe I'd remember."

"Pa-bo!" the voice said.

"Do I even want to—"

"It means stupid," Helen said.

"You're awake," Max said.

"How do you know that?" Yong asked.

"I am not stupid," Helen answered.

Max wondered what that made him.

The dog's started to bark, then whimpered almost in unison, and quieted.

"Why do they do that?" he asked out loud.

"Do what?" Helen asked.

"Stop barking right after they start."

"Bark collars, probably. Or a similar device. A tone we can't hear or something."

Max turned left and right. Still couldn't make out anything. There wasn't enough light for his eyes to adjust.

Tried to move his feet and found he could.

He was still secured to the chair, but they'd been moved. Whatever they'd been given must have been very effective.

He attempted to lift the chair from the floor, but it must have been bolted down.

Max gave up struggling.

"Helen?" he asked.

"Yes Max?"

"Where were you? When you were missing? What happened?"

"I don't really remember."

"Nothing?"

"Not much. I-my daughter. I remember two men. They came in the house and shot the dog first thing. I heard the shot from upstairs."

She got quiet, and he heard sobs.

"Then I heard my daughter..."

"You don't have to..." But Max stopped himself. She didn't have to, but he would bet she would feel better talking to someone. He hadn't told anyone his end of the story since the police report.

Yet he'd gone over it in his head again and again. Wondering if he could have done anything differently.

"Yes, I do," she said. "It's important that you know. In case, you know, Jenny went through the same thing."

There was a pause, and Max almost spoke.

"I heard my daughter," she said, her voice stronger now. "I heard her say, 'No.' Then I heard her scream."

"I ran down the stairs. There was blood, blood everywhere. I must have screamed. I don't know. I'm shocked my neighbors did not hear me, call the cops."

"Maybe they did."

"Maybe. I ran to the kitchen, and something hit me in the back of the head. It hurt, but then I felt a prick in my arm. The next thing I knew, I woke up in a cage."

"A cage?" Max asked. "Where?"

"I don't know."

"What happened next?"

"It was awful. The first memory I have was at least a few days later, although time seemed to blur. The first thing that happened was—"

Her words cut off. The dogs started to bark again, and then whimpered and stopped.

The lights came on, and Max closed his eyes against them. They hurt, clear back into his brain.

"Time to go," he heard a voice say.

Then Helen screamed.

***

Max didn't think.

He popped his eyes open, still squinted against the pain the light brought.

Saw Helen's eyes wide, fixed on something ahead of her.

Turned to look and saw a man with a dog.

Jennifer. Jenny. Helen's dog that was not her dog.

The man was choking the animal with a leash. The dog's tongue hung out of her mouth sideways. The whites of her eyes showed, and her ears were flat against her skull.

It made Max mad, and so he tried to stand again. At first the chair didn't budge, but something gave in his shoulder, and he heard a splintering sound as the chair broke free of the floor.

He rushed ahead, seeing movement from the corner of his eye.

As much as his eyes had been unable to adjust to the dark, they were rapidly recovering in the light, although they watered excessively, and he needed to wipe the tears from them.

Instead, he blinked repeatedly.

The movement came from one of the goons rushing in at him from the side.

"Watch out!" Helen screamed.

Max was already watching and moving.

Just before the man reached him, Max spun, hitting him in the thigh with the chair leg. The man dropped to one knee, grabbing the spot he'd been struck.

Seeing him down, Max did the only thing he could think of: he sat the chair, and then himself, down on the man's outstretched leg.

He heard a loud snap, followed by a high-pitched scream. Not stopping to look, he launched to his feet again and ran toward the man strangling the dog.

The man dropped the leash and turned to face him. Max didn't slow, but bowled into him like a linebacker, lowering his shoulder, and hoping he would roll to his feet.

He struck the smaller man dead center in the chest, and they both went over. Instead of a graceful somersault, Max landed on his side, and another jolt of pain shot into his already aching shoulder.

He shrugged it off, rolled to his knees, and then struggled to his feet, hunched over by the chair, ready to meet any opposition.

There was no need. Jennifer has sufficiently recovered to growl at her assailant. As Max watched him grab for her leash again, she spun and sank her teeth into his hand.

The man howled, and struck at her, but the dog was quicker, and let her jaws open, dodging the blow. The man kicked out, his eyes wide, and she sunk her teeth into his calf. He fell to the floor, reaching for the wound.

The dog bounded away again.

Max rushed forward, and spun, striking the man with the only weapon he had handy, the chair still attached to his back.

Sharp pain shot through his shoulder and his chest as the legs struck the fallen, screaming man in the head, but the noise stopped with the blow.

Max backed up, panting, and sat down. The only two men in sight were on the ground. One was sobbing, grabbing what certainly appeared to be a broken leg. The other lay unconscious and bleeding.

Jennifer, the dog, came to his side. He wondered if that was her real name. Helen had used a fake one, there was no reason to assume the dog's was any more real.

Except the dog responded to it.

"Good girl," he said, wishing he could pat her head.

She looked up at him panting. They'd heard dogs here, there had to be kennels somewhere. With water.

Max pondered their situation. He needed to get free of the chair soon. Get the others free as well and leave.

There had been seven men before, including Director Atwill.

Two were here, one likely out for a while, the other on the permanent disabled list, although his voice still worked, should he choose to use it.

Max wondered if he had keys to the cuffs and decided to find out.

He stood again, in the half crouch the chair allowed, and hurried over to the man, sitting next to him. Max extended his foot and pressed it against the man's injured leg.

The man howled.

"Shhh," Max said. "Keep it down. You got a key to these cuffs?"

"Fuck you," came the strained response. Max looked over at Helen and Yong, sitting in chairs still attached to the floor. He had no leverage, no way to free them until he was loose himself.

Max eased up. "You want some help? You are bleeding pretty good there. Maybe arterial. You don't, you might die."

The man tried to stand, his face twisted in rage.

Max turned the chair, and sat down, the legs straddling his chest.

"How about we start over? Keys."

The man looked up at Max, then at his feet, on either side of his head.

Max tapped his feet. "That's right. I can't hit you. But I can kick the shit out of you. Keys."

Inexplicably the man smiled up at him.

"Fuck you!" he yelled. In one motion, he used one arm to push the chair up to one side, putting Max off balance. With his other hand the man reached for Max's ankle.

A second too late, Max yelled and tried to push back down.

The man had his gun. He pulled the hammer of the .38 back and fired.

Max felt the bullet whiz by his left ear, and instinctively rolled to the right. He crashed onto his shoulder again and felt a pop. It had separated or something, and the pain was incredible. But he had to move.

Move or die.

He rolled over onto his knees again, managing to get to his feet, seeing purple and green pain spots invade his vision.

It blurred, cleared, blurred again. He blinked.

Waving the gun wildly, the man fired again.

Helen screamed, this time in pain.

Max turned to see a hole appear in her shoulder.

He did the only thing he could think of. Launched himself, chair and all, at the man on the floor.

Felt the hot metal of the barrel against his bare arm. Then it moved away and the man below him cried out.

Max heard another gunshot, and then his head hit the floor.

First came shadows.

Pain.

Blackness.

Sleep.

HARVESTED

Chapter Twenty-Four

Daggers of light pierced his eyelids, making his head throb.

He could hear his heartbeat in his ears.

Max took that as a good sign. He was alive.

Awareness came in stages.

He again found himself sitting upright. Now his ankles were bound as well, he assumed to the legs of the chair.

Around his wrists, he still felt the steel of cuffs. He could move his left arm, but only slightly. His arms must now be bound to the arms of the chair.

He tried to move his right arm, and his right shoulder immediately caught fire. Determined to keep quiet, a moan escaped his lips anyway.

"Ah. Mr. Boucher. You are awake. Good."

Max opened his eyes, blinking. They adjusted quickly this time. He hadn't been in darkness for nearly as long.

He was in the same room, but the chair was a different one. Much larger bolts secured it to the floor. Clearly, he was in a different area, because there were several kennels up against the wall in front of him, each at least eight feet tall. They were rectangular, at least twenty feet by ten. Inside each, seven to ten dogs lay on the floor, most motionless.

At first, he thought they might be dead. But then he saw an ear move, a chest rise and fall here and there.

He looked to the right, and the comfort he'd felt went away. There were two stations, with a surgical table and instruments to measure vitals. A surgical team of four manned both. As he watched, a member of the second team opened a freezer. Inside he could see rows of bags, all with bloody objects inside. Organs.

"I figured you might want to see our operation, from start," the director stepped into his view, and gestured at the cages, "to the end." Max felt ready to puke, but also suddenly recognized him. It must be the different light.

"You were the vagrant. Outside Dr. Gamble's clinic."

The man simply smiled. The dog on the second table whimpered loudly, and his chest rose and fell rapidly. Monitors beeped.

The doctors, or whoever surrounded him, mumbled to each other, and went about mechanical tasks, ones that looked oddly similar to what he'd seen on television medical dramas.

He turned his gaze back to the director, keeping it neutral, trying not to show weakness. But he was not hopeful for escape. He held no illusions that this man had any intention of letting him or the others go.

The others.

He looked around.

"Where are they?"

"You mean your friends?" the man said. "We decided perhaps it would be best to separate you, at least for the moment."

"Helen needs—"

"Ah, yes. The one you shot."

"I didn't shoot her."

"But it was your weapon."

"One of your goons took it from me."

"That will be most difficult to prove, Mr. Boucher. He's dead."

"Dead?"

"Turns out you shot him too. After you went crazy and wounded your friend."

"But I didn't."

"I've been debating about you Mr. Boucher. What to do with you."

"Killing me seems easy enough."

"Someone might come looking for you. Unless, of course, they found you."

"Found me?"

"Perhaps found you in a compromising position. With two bodies. And the weapon that killed them."

"No one will believe it. I'll tell them the truth."

"Ah, that's the sad part. You were a troubled man. Upset at your wife's disappearance, the murder of your family. You managed to hold it together for three years before you snapped. Killed two suspects in a case you were involved in, and then turned the weapon on yourself."

"I have friends who won't buy that story."

"They will, when the evidence tells them it's true. When you have the gun residue on your hands. When one of the analysts they have brought in, if they even bother, proves beyond a shadow of a doubt you shot yourself."

"How will he do that?"

"Because you're going to, Mr. Boucher. And I will provide you with the incentive to do so."

"Call me Max."

"What?"

"Knock off the Mr. Boucher bullshit. If you think you know me well enough to motivate me to shoot myself, at least call me by my first name."

"Okay, Max." The man bent close. Max could smell his sweat. The tart smell of fish on his breath. "I'll be back soon."

The man disappeared, and a moment later Max heard a door open and shut. He looked to the right.

The surgeons did not even spare him a glance, just continued their work. They appeared to be almost done with the patient, judging by what he'd helped Helen do previously.

The dogs still slept, or at least just lay in the cages.

Waiting for their organs to be harvested, and then to live or die. The surgeons, for that was the only way he could think of them, finished what they were doing, clearly in a hurry. One placed whatever they had removed from the dog in a bag and put it in the freezer nearby. Surely, they had to ship those soon. He'd always gotten the impression that such things were time sensitive. On TV, helicopters took tissue on dry ice miles to patients desperately clinging to life.

Unless these organs were for a different purpose. Experiments, maybe.

Another of the men in scrubs picked up the dog. He put it in a kennel on the end, one where all the dogs inside had similar bandages around their mid sections.

Then a buzzer sounded. Several of the dogs woke, started barking, whimpered and settled back down.

The men took off bloodied scrubs and threw them in a red hamper, clearly designed for the purpose. They filed out of the room in the same direction the first man had gone, hardly sparing him a glance.

Max heard the door open and close several times.

Then he was alone.

Except for the dogs.

Movement caught his eye down on one end. A small heeler mix was more alert than the rest. He was up on his hind legs trying to open the latch of the kennel.

A pin held the latch in place, but it wasn't locked. As he watched the dog nosed the pin over and over, and it edged closer to falling on the floor.

Come on, boy, Max said to himself.

He had no idea how one dog getting loose might help, but it was the only hope he saw in the room.

***

The pin clattered to the floor.

A few other dogs stirred, then settled. They must be sedated, Max decided. He thought he recognized one on the end. He'd bet it was Eddie's dog. It was not yet bandaged.

It was a tragedy they would both die here.

Then as the heeler stood on its hind legs and nosed it, the gate clanged. The latch moved up and fell back into place.

The heeler tried again.

The latch stayed up for a second, and the gate swung outward, open.

The dog darted out and danced a circle. Max noted he did not bark. Then Max recognized him, too. He was one of the two taken from Dr. Gamble's during the robbery. He didn't have any bandages on him yet either.

The collar around his neck looked like one of the anti-bark ones he'd seen. Once he'd witnessed a demonstration, he never had the heart to use one on Houston. Dogs were supposed to bark, at least sometimes.

Clearly the heeler was clever, and a fast learner.

The dog darted back into the kennel, nudging some of his companions with his nose. Several woke up, groggily lifting their heads. A few perked at the open door and stood. Several simply laid their heads back down in a resigned sleep.

Shit, Max thought. If only he were smart enough to bring me a set of cuff keys.

He watched as the heeler led those who were awake toward the door. Occasionally one would wander or lag behind, and the heeler would circle around the back of the group, effectively herding them forward.

Max was so transfixed he didn't hear the door open.

The heeler charged the first man through, knocking him over. The other dogs raced past him, out the door and into the hall.

The man the heeler had knocked over managed to find his feet.

Reaching into his pocket, he drew out a syringe.

Max tugged at the chair, his restraints, but there was no way he could get free this time. The chair was stronger, better secured.

He watched in horror as man and dog circled. As they did, the last of the awakened dogs went through the door, and it clicked shut.

It must be thick, the walls to this area nearly soundproof, because he couldn't hear a thing beyond it.

The man lashed out with the needle, and the heeler dodged. His tongue hung out, panting. He must be in need of water, or still suffering the effects of earlier sedatives.

He appeared to be tiring fast.

"Hey!" Max yelled in desperation.

The man looked over at him, and the heeler attacked.

Canine teeth sunk into the flesh of the arm holding the syringe, and the man's shirt immediately turned red. He growled, the drugs dropping to the floor.

With his uninjured hand, he struck out at the attacking dog.

He landed one blow, and then a second.

The heeler fell to the ground and rolled away.

Holding his wounded arm, clearly angry, the man followed.

He struck out with his foot once, twice, connecting both times.

The heeler yelped with the first.

When the second landed, the dog simply fell to the floor, motionless.

The man grinned.

"Serves you right, you fuck!" he told the dog.

He spun toward Max, blood spurting from the wound on his arm. His skin was pale, and his breath came in short gasps.

"I'll deal with you later, asshole."

"I look forward to it," Max said calmly.

"We'll see." The man smiled. He turned and spotted the open kennel. He walked over and closed it, without replacing the pin.

Max figured if he had bent over to retrieve it, he would probably pass out.

When he turned back around there was even more blood on the front of his shirt, and his face was sheet white.

The man stumbled toward the door, nearly falling twice, and managed to get it open.

Max heard him cry out as soon as he reached the hallway, but the door closed, cutting off the sound.

He looked at the blood on the floor. The fallen heeler. The cage, not as secure as it had been.

Insanely, the dog's escapade had given him hope.

Max smiled to himself. He'd find a way out of this. He knew it.

He glanced at the heeler one more time. To his astonishment, the dog moved. Slowly, he stood, panting and clearly in pain.

The animal moved toward Max, and he heard a low growl in the back of its throat.

HARVESTED

Chapter Twenty-Five

The heeler advanced, and Max felt even more trapped, his only recourse was comforting words.

"Easy, boy," he said. "I'm one of the good guys."

The dog looked unconvinced. Maybe it wasn't a boy.

"Girl?" he tried. "Easy girl?"

The dog stopped, but its hackles were still up, ears perked.

"Easy. Good dog," Max said. "Good dog."

The words eventually seemed to register. The dog stopped growling and went back to panting.

He could see the blood on her snout, recognized the smell of fear.

"It's okay," he tried to soothe, frustrated by the fact he couldn't gesture. Couldn't kneel to her level, show her he wasn't a threat.

She took a few last tentative steps and laid down beside his chair.

Damn, he thought. What now?

Max hung his head, resting. Knowing the peace would be disrupted and soon.

He was not wrong. A minute, maybe five passed. He could not be sure. He almost felt as if he'd dozed off.

The door burst open. For a moment, he found himself largely ignored.

If he'd been free, or had any hope of freedom, that would have been his moment to spring. To escape. But this was not the movies.

All he could do was watch.

Someone re-secured the kennel with the pin. Another man checked all of the gates.

Dogs barked, quieted, barked again.

A man moved close enough to lift the heeler from the floor. The dog did not move, didn't fight or attack.

It must finally have succumbed to exhaustion.

A moment later, a man in blue scrubs slipped a syringe into the flesh near its neck.

The same man carried the dog out of sight.

The surgeons were back, but not working. They were watching the others rush around in panic. One of the dogs still laying on a table stirred, whined, and went quiet.

The door opened again, and three men entered, each with a dog on a leash. They put them back into the kennel.

Max watched it all, studying the movement of every one of them.

Trying to determine a way to kill them all.

How many dogs had escaped thanks to the heeler? He thought more than three. Five, maybe?

Good. Maybe two were still out there somewhere, raising hell.

"What about him?" one man said.

"Leave him be. The boss has special plans for him."

"Too bad," the other one replied. "I'd love to kick his ass."

"In your dreams, motherfucker," Max said.

"What did you say?" the man turned slowly.

"I said, in your dreams. Are you deaf and ugly?"

Max knew getting him hyped up was a bad idea, and he did it anyway.

"I should take you right here," the man growled.

The second man came back over. "Trust me, he's not worth it. We'll have a chance later, if we want."

"Yeah" the man smiled. "I look forward to it."

"Me too," Max replied, wondering just what the man meant.

A chance at him later?

Was that going to be the motive he was offered to shoot himself? If it was, the man behind this was a poor judge of character.

Max didn't believe that. Something else was in the works.

He wished he knew where Helen was, wished he could be sure she was okay.

Even wished he knew where Yong was. Max thought at the end of all this, he might owe the man an apology, if he lasted that long.

The door burst open behind him. He heard the now familiar voice.

"What in hell happened in here?"

Several voices answered at once.

"One at a time!" the voice said, and everyone went silent.

The voices settled, and Max could only assume each was telling his version of the story.

"Fine, fine," he finally said. Max wished he could see them, read their body language. But he could only see those still in front of him, in his line of vision, and turning around and craning his head might be a very bad idea.

"Get the dogs ready. And the shipment. It needs to leave on schedule."

Men rushed to tasks, and then Max's view was blocked by a very large man.

Probably the largest he'd ever seen outside of television shows.

He looked like the final fighter in so many martial arts movies, square jawed and well-muscled.

"Get him up," the voice said. "It is time."

The man silently obeyed, first kneeling to release his feet.

Max flexed them. Thought of kicking out, but the timing felt wrong.

Still, deep inside, an anger simmered, one that told him to act. He kept it in check, fighting impatience.

He felt the man's strength when he released one wrist, left the cuffs hanging, and then released the right cuff from the arm of the chair.

The man then secured Max's hands together in front of him. When he jerked him to his feet, Max's right shoulder erupted in pain again.

He needed to do something, but nothing he did would be easy, and anything might get him killed.

Max allowed himself to be led to the door and into the hall, feeling like he had no choice at all.

The big man did not smile or speak.

They went past two doors, and then Max was forced into the third.

It was small, the ceiling low, with two barred windows high above.

There were only two chairs secured to the floor in the center. Yong was imprisoned in one, similarly to how Max had just been secured.

In the other sat Helen. Or rather, she slumped. Her hair hung over her face, and the skin he could see was ghostly pale.

Her left shoulder was in a crude bandage, one he assumed had once been white. It was now crimson.

"Enjoy," the large man said. "It will be over soon."

He left, and Max heard the door lock.

Hands cuffed in front of him, he looked first at Yong, who looked back at him without a word.

He looked at Helen, and then asked Yong. "Is she—?" he asked.

"I think so. I hear her breathing from time to time. She hasn't spoken though."

Max rushed to her side. He knelt, and with both hands felt for a pulse. Found one, weak and thready.

"She needs a doctor," Max said, and felt stupid for saying it.

"Then get her one," Yong said.

Max looked around the room for hope. Anything that might offer some salvation.

Looked at both chairs, and the bolts securing them to the floor.

Damn.

Looked at Yong, studying his clothing.

Nothing.

Looked again at Helen, head to toe.

Then wondered.

Went to her shirt, and with both hands held close together by the cuffs, unbuttoned her shirt. Looked closely at her bra.

"Sorry Helen," he said, and undid the clasp in the front. Max tried not to look but was unable to help himself.

Saw the opening in the fabric around the cup.

Tugged, and Helen moaned. The strap had to be rubbing against the wound in her shoulder.

But he had it started. He worked, trying to jostle her as little as possible.

Apologized twice more when she moaned.

Then had the underwire from her bra in his hands. A long, thin piece of metal.

Took the end of it and bent it at a 90-degree angle.

Picked first the left cuff, and then the right, taking him an eternal minute and a half.

He hurried over and knelt beside Yong to free him.

As he was picking the second cuff to free his hands, he heard a key turn in the door.

"Give the wire to me," Yong said.

Max did and stood to face whoever was coming through the door, flexing his right shoulder as he did.

At the slightest twitch in it Max winced.

This was probably going to hurt, but he was out of options.

***

Surprise was about the only thing on Max's side and he intended to use it as much as he could.

The door opened, and a man stepped through.

Max hoped it was not the big man who had led him into the room. Maybe he should have prayed after all, because it was.

Using his good left arm, he grabbed the man and pulled him inside. As the huge body stumbled, he stuck his foot out, accelerating his fall further. Letting go, he struck out with his left fist striking with rabbit punches to the man's kidneys.

Or so he hoped.

His knuckles immediately hurt. Hitting his assailant's body was like punching a concrete wall.

The man managed to keep his feet, and turned his full rage toward Max.

Damn.

A wide, slow punch came, and he ducked under it, stepping closer instead of away. He struck out again, the jab finding the man's midsection. Stomping on the man's right foot, Max spun away.

It was like he was poking a bear with a stick. His assailant turned and roared, coming at him again, this time grasping lower.

Max danced away, looking for something in the small room, anything that might serve as a weapon.

There was nothing.

So he threw himself to the ground on his left side.

The charging man tripped over him. His boot struck Max in the ribs and he swore he heard a loud crack.

Incredible pain followed.

Jesus, this guy was strong.

He struggled to get a breath but managed to spin onto his hands and knees.

The large man lay on the floor but was already moving to get up.

Max crawled forward, up his back, trying to push him down. His assailant tried to stand, pushing him upward. Max pressed his knee into the middle of his back, and then threw a fist into his side over and over again.

He heard the grunt he was looking for as the man's body pitched forward again.

Max unbuckled and pulled off his belt in one smooth motion, tossing it forward around the man's neck.

He grabbed the other side with his right arm and pulled for all he was worth.

The man's body bucked under him like an eight second rodeo bull. Max struggled to hold on, his right shoulder screaming in pain.

Slowly, the belt slipped out of his hands. He was losing his grip.

The large man made it to his knees and managed to get one foot under him.

Then his other foot.

He stood, and Max found himself hanging on to the belt, dangling from the man's back.

Then two large hands grabbed the belt, pulling it forward, dragging Max with it.

The man spun, and Max saw Helen flash before his eyes.

Then an empty chair.

Yong was free.

The man jerked on the belt, and Max lost his grip with his aching right arm. Holding on with only his left, he was thrown to the floor. He landed on his right side and groaned. He had to get up.

Then he heard a loud "oof."

Then a clatter, and a loud thud.

Someone was tugging at the belt he still held in his left hand.

"Let it go!" he heard Yong say.

He opened his hand and felt the leather slip free of his grip.

He then struggled to his hands and knees, favoring his right arm.

Looking over, he saw Yong was riding the large man, the belt around his neck.

Only it was working. The man was on his knees, his face red.

"Max," Yong called out. "Help!"

Max did not know what he could do, or how he might help. He felt so weak. So inadequate.

But he managed to stand. Made his way across the floor. Pulled back his left foot. Kicked out at the man's gut.

The bulky assailant fell, Yong on top of him. Yong sat on the middle of his back, strangling him.

Max walked around stepping between his legs and swinging his right foot back.

He kicked the gasping man square in the groin, causing him to yelp, then stop struggling.

Yong didn't stop his efforts.

Max staggered, falling back heavily against the wall, striking his right shoulder and nearly blacking out.

He was sure the man was dead, but he could barely stand himself. Reinforcements would be coming when he didn't show up wherever he had been supposed to take them.

"Yong!" he yelled. "Yong! Enough. We have to go."

Yong slowly responded, letting the belt drop to the floor before standing, breathing hard.

"What about her?" he nodded to Helen.

"We'll have to come back," Max said.

As pale as she was, he thought it might already be too late.

As he went to step over the unmoving man, he looked down.

He recognized the handle of his .38, tucked into the back of his belt.

Pulling it out, he popped open the cylinder.

How nice. It had been reloaded.

He had six shots again.

"Let's get them," he said to Yong, suddenly feeling stronger.

Yong looked at the gun and nodded.

Max held the weapon in his left hand hoped he could shoot accurately with it.

He also hoped someone had heard something, and help might be on the way.

Stopping himself, he recalled the way his hopes were working out lately and whispered a prayer instead.

HARVESTED

Chapter Twenty-Six

Max pulled the door open, and found a dog staring up at him.

It barked, then whimpered as a light on its collar went red.

He thought of setting the rest of the dogs free.

It might cause confusion, but if a door was open, they also might just run off.

Then locating them could be a nightmare. Owners, if the dogs had them, would be disappointed. Including Eddie. And the two from the clinic. He hoped the heeler was okay.

Max hesitated while weighing his options.

He should not have.

A man ran into the hall, spotted, him, and turned back the other way.

Max looked down at the dog at his feet, with no idea if he would listen or not.

"Get him!" he said, pointing.

The dog hesitated, and Max reached down, spinning the offending no-bark collar around, finding the buckle, and undoing it. He tossed it aside.

The dog barked, then winced in anticipation. The animal's eyes widened with pleasure when no shock came.

It turned and ran down the hall, barking the entire way.

"We have to let the dogs free," Max said to Yong, making the decision as he spoke.

"You think that best?" Yong said. His eyes were wide, and he spit as he spoke, clearly still angry and spoiling for a fight.

"I don't know," Max said, and hurried back down the hall to the room containing the kennels before he could change his mind.

Once he entered the room, Max opened the first gate, and began to undo collars.

A few of the dogs got up, shook themselves, and wandered out.

Most still laid there, in drugged stupor.

He moved to the second kennel and the third, with the same result.

Opened the final door.

In the end about a dozen dogs wandered the room sleepily.

The rest still lay in the cages, but at least without the collars, and the doors open.

Max turned around.

Yong was gone.

Max ran out and found the hall empty.

He ran the direction the dog had gone as fast as he could, his legs feeling like lead.

He nearly tripped as he rounded the corner but kept going. He had no idea where the hall led.

There were at least five men here somewhere. Where would they be, if not with the dogs?

Preparing for transport. Hadn't that been what the man said before? Preparing them for transport? And prepping the shipment? Preparing to take them where? Were they moving them all the way across the country to Maine?

There was so much he didn't know. So little time.

Max rounded another corner and saw Yong.

He was facing a smaller, faster man, and they were engaged in hand to hand combat, so intensely they did not even see Max or hear him arrive.

Max did the only thing he could think of. He pulled the .38. Aimed and said two words:

"Hold it!"

Yong stopped to look at him.

His opponent did not. Time slowed.

A first approached Yong's throat, striking it, hard.

His Adam's apple appeared to collapse, and he drew in a sharp, high pitched breath.

Max took aim and fired. One minute the small man was grinning in triumph, fist extended, the next a hole appeared in his throat.

Now the air filled with wheezing and gurgling, as two men struggled to live, suffering from two very different wounds.

Max ignored the other man and rushed to Yong's side.

Max would not call him his friend, exactly.

They weren't even on the same side, necessarily, but he still deserved a chance to live.

Max sat him up.

"Deep breaths," he said. "Slow and easy."

"Gack!" Yong said. At least that meant he was getting air. "Gack!" he tried again and raised his arm.

Max felt something strike him in the center of his back, and rolled away, turning his head to face his next challenge.

He bumped his right shoulder on the wall and felt the fire start all over again.

As he looked up, green and purple spots danced in his vision.

He saw two men, the large man he thought Yong had killed, and a squat one staring at him.

The smaller man held a pistol and raised it.

Max fired from the hip, instinctively, and then heard a loud pop.

The fire in his shoulder got more intense, if that was even possible.

He heard a roar of rage. The voice sounded familiar, yet distant.

He fired again, once, twice, three times, and then spun away on the floor, looking for shelter, finding nothing but open tile.

No one followed, and he looked back to see two bodies.

Two down. Two to go.

He tried to find his feet, and found he could, but barely. He fought to remain conscious.

Warm liquid poured down his right side.

It felt odd, almost comforting.

Max stumbled down the hall, opposite of the way he'd come.

In his left hand he held his pistol, his right dangling at his side.

Max had become a hunter. Wounded, angry, and dangerous.

***

Max limped around the corner to the right.

The hall seemed to simply run around the central warehouse.

Or rooms. There had to be at least two, right?

But maybe not. The first one had been artificially created, with a tarp or something. To hide what was on the other side.

Then there had to be a loading dock or something. Somewhere the last men were getting ready to transport the dogs.

He had to find it.

But the hall kept tilting. His vision kept getting blurry, the fluorescent lights in the ceiling getting crooked, moving diagonally and then switching directions.

Max wanted to say there was something wrong with the building, but knew it was something wrong with him.

The wetness on his side was growing. He knew it meant he needed to find some help.

But help would be impossible if he didn't stop these men. And he didn't see how he could not stop them.

The dogs. Everything. He couldn't let them get away with it.

He stumbled on. There was a door up ahead, and it looked close at first, but it must have been farther ahead than he thought. It was taking a long time to get there.

He heard a helicopter, rotors approaching. The shipment. That's what they meant.

A man came through the door he'd been struggling to reach. Looked at him, puzzled at first. Then recognition crossed his face, and his mouth tightened.

He came towards Max, menace in his eyes.

The gun still hung in his left hand.

He wanted to use it, but even with his diminished capacity, knew he could not fire effectively until the man got closer.

Hell, even then he had his doubts about hitting anything.

First one figure approached him, then two.

He blinked the tears away, and there was one again. Then it divided again into two.

Which one should he shoot? When?

Then the figure grabbed his right wrist. Solidified.

Max brought the gun up, pushing it into the man's belly, and fired. There was a loud explosion.

He pulled the trigger again. Click.

Again.

Click.

Dropped it. The gun was empty.

The other man looked shocked. He stared straight ahead, not seeing Max at all, but still gripping his wrist.

He fell backward, pulling Max with him. Max could not pull his arm free, or resist. He was too weak, and fell forward, on top of the man. He could no longer feel his right arm.

His vision was filled with a single white tile. Red liquid crept across it.

What is that? he thought to himself.

Then he heard a sound. A click as the door at the end of the hall opened again. He tried to raise his head. See who it was. Director Atwill stepped through. He stared at first, a look of anger on his face.

Max looked at him and tried to say something.

Found his mouth filled with cotton, and liquid with an iron taste. He spit and tried again.

"Mr. Boucher," the man said. "At last, you have lived up to your name."

He smiled as Max managed to free his wrist from the other man's grasp. He crawled back, struggling. He reached the wall, tried to push himself up using it.

Slid back down.

Spat again, and watched as something dark red exited his mouth, and splattered on the tile, a new puddle forming.

Fuck.

Tried again.

The director stepped forward, grinning.

Then looked beyond Max, a look of surprise on his face.

"What are you doing here?" he asked.

A small pop answered, and a hole appeared in his thigh. He dropped to one knee but looked back up with a snarl. Reaching in his jacket, he pulled out a small pistol. Fired back the direction Max could not see.

The pop of his gun was followed by a squeal.

A feminine squeal.

Then another pop came from that direction, and a hole appeared in the center of the director's forehead.

He fell forward, unmoving.

Max had to see behind him. Struggled to spin his body around, the ceiling spinning.

Helen was laying just a few feet away. She looked horrid. Her shoulder was a mess of both drying and oozing blood. She had a new hole in her thigh, bleeding profusely.

"Helen," he said weakly. "How—?" Max settled into a fit of coughing.

Tried to crawl closer.

He saw her lips move.

"Max," she said, almost a whisper.

"Helen," he said. "Hang on. Hang on. I'll go for help."

Her mouth tried to smile. Her lips only rose on one side. The eye on that side closed at the same time.

"You are in no shape to get help," she whispered, a little louder.

"Hang on," he said again. The wall was getting harder to hang on to. It kept tilting.

"I don't think I can, Max. But Max, there's something you need to know."

"Yes, Helen?"

"She was supposed to replace me."

"Jenny?"

"Yes. But she fought them. She wouldn't just do what they wanted even though I told her to."

"What happened? Helen?" Her head rolled back on her neck, and new strength flowed into him. He made it closer to her. Tried to reach out with his right hand. Could not.

He was laying on his left.

"Helen, tell me. What happened to Jenny?"

She shook her head. "She didn't make it. They—they killed her."

"Helen?" Her eyes were closed, although he could still see the rise and fall of her chest.

"Arrrrrgggghhhhhh!" he roared.

Then heard sirens.

Sirens. He hoped they weren't too late.

Then changed his mind. Instead of just hoping, Max rolled off his left side leaning against the wall, which still seemed determined to dump him onto the floor.

Took his left hand, and carelessly crossed himself.

Prayed they weren't too late, and Helen would be okay.

Prayed he would be too and could learn more from her. The fact that Jenny was gone seemed both impossible and true at the same time. His eyes filled with tears, and his chest rose and fell with heavy sobs. The movement hurt, but he couldn't stop.

He closed his eyes, as he'd been taught in Sunday school. "Dear God," he breathed.

Then fell into unconsciousness.

Chapter Twenty-Seven

Tony was the first one through the door. He didn't even belong on this task force or this investigation.

But he'd insisted on being here.

The team split up, one team to the front, the other covering the rear. Four other officers covered the big warehouse door.

He followed the SWAT officers into the front door which led into a hallway with door after door. Inside the second were about eight dogs. The lead officer tried to close the door quickly, but a lone mutt managed to escape.

The dog ran past Tony, then stopped, turned, and trotted to his heels. Tony ignored him.

Around the next corner, they found the first body.

The man lay on the floor in a puddle of blood. He appeared to have been shot.

It was the first of three. Most were in the hall, on the floor. One was slumped against the wall.

The dog with him lifted his leg and peed on the body.

Tony did not pause. In other circumstances, he might have laughed. But not this time.

Max was here somewhere, he knew it.

In his inside jacket pocket were two envelopes, one from Yong Myung to someone Tony assumed was his daughter.

The other was thicker.

Filled with blueprints.

Invoices.

Shipping records, bills of lading.

And this address.

Tony found the envelopes in Max's car. This is where he would be, so he came right away. There was no dusting for prints, time to investigate.

Max had been missing, out of contact, and his phone went directly to voice mail. As a result, Tony had put out a BOLO on his car.

Patrol officers had found it fairly quickly. He opened it with the extra keys he still carried from when they were partners.

He'd simply reacted and called in a favor.

His partner was in trouble. Technically his ex-partner, but fuck semantics.

Around the next corner. A blond female was lying against the wall, slumped over. One of the officers knelt. Checked for a pulse.

Nodded, but waffled his hand.

So-so.

Came to another body and performed another check.

A slashing motion across the throat.

Done.

Then Tony spotted him.

Max was laying across another body. Blood flowed from a wound in his shoulder. Slowly, but it flowed.

Dead people's blood didn't flow.

Tony knelt beside him.

"Max. Max." He repeated it, but Max did not respond. Did not hear him.

"We need a bus in here!" he hissed.

"We have to clear the building first," an officer said. "We're almost there."

One man stayed behind. The officer laid the blond back on the floor. Took out a basic first aid kit and started an evaluation.

Tony checked Max over. Gunshot wound to the shoulder. Another to the leg. Right shoulder looked funny too, maybe dislocated.

He didn't dare move him but checked gently for other bleeding.

Found none.

Sat back against the wall and looked over at the officer with the woman.

His face looked grim. He had a packet of clotting powder in his hand but had not opened it.

"How bad?" Tony asked.

"Bad. She needs fluids. Probably blood." He held up the packet. "This might do more harm than good."

Tony nodded. Closed his eyes, and leaned back, silently praying, remembering his Sunday lessons as a child.

A new set of sirens rose in the distance, and from the direction the men had gone he saw uniformed men rushing in, but not cops.

They were EMT's, with stretchers. They scattered, checking bodies.

Two came straight to Tony, who pointed to Max.

Two more knelt next to the blond.

He watched as they log rolled her, put her onto a stretcher.

One of the men started an I.V., before putting a bag over her mouth and nose, pumping it repeatedly.

Max got the same treatment. Without the bag. His breathing was okay, apparently.

As they wheeled him past Tony, his eyes opened, went wide, then closed again.

Tony followed the men out to two waiting ambulances.

They drove off, sirens wailing, lights flashing.

"Detective?" an officer said from behind him.

"Yeah?" he said, turning.

"You gotta see this. Follow me."

As he ducked inside, an animal control van screeched to a halt outside the big door.

A car followed closely and a woman in scrubs got out. Ignoring them, Tony ducked inside.

***

Light.

Again, the stabbing. Why couldn't they just let him sleep?

A beeping of some sort. An alarm. He didn't remember that tone on his phone.

His phone?

Hadn't that prick thrown it away?

Memories flooded back, and he tried to sit up.

But couldn't. There was something across his chest.

Just the flexing of his muscles at the attempt sent a fire into his shoulder.

Max heard himself groan. Tried to take a mental inventory.

Left side okay. Not great, but okay.

He moved his left hand, flexed the fingers. They felt funny, almost numb. He could move his left leg, but not much. It felt restrained.

That knee hurt, a low, aching pain.

Continuing to inventory his body, he tried to move his right leg.

There was pain. Excruciating pain.

He moaned again.

Then he heard shuffling, some kind of commotion.

Max opened his eyes, and blinked, clearing them.

His right arm was hung somehow in the air, and so was his right leg. Both were in casts. The right side of his chest was also covered with a bandage.

He was in a hospital.

A nurse entered the room. Rushed to his side.

"Glad to see you back, Mr. Boucher."

"Call me Max," he croaked.

She looked at him, blinked.

He tried to speak again. Started to cough and set his shoulder on fire again.

"Easy," she said. "Relax."

She brought a water glass towards his mouth, a small straw sticking out of it. He took a drink and found heaven. He wanted more, and tried for it, but only got a little before she pulled it away.

"A little at a time," she smiled.

He liked her smile.

"Call me Max," he said, his voice stronger this time. "I insist all women who have seen me naked call me Max."

She giggled. "Tony warned me you would be trouble."

Max sobered. She reminded him of Jenny.

Jenny. Helen.

"How is the woman that came in with me?" he managed.

"Rest, Mr.—Max. When you wake next, you can have company."

"Did she make it?"

"Rest," she said. She took a syringe and slid it into something sticking out of the I.V. running into his arm.

Max suddenly had a metallic taste in his mouth and fell back into sleep.

***

He blinked awake, feeling better, but his mouth still felt full of cotton.

He was sitting up more. He could actually see around the room.

Tony sat in the corner, and looked up from a book he was reading, a book with a UFO on the front, and the simple title *Bob*.

He closed it and stood.

"Welcome back, Max," he said.

Max grinned at his friend, then got serious.

"What happened Tony?"

"We found your car and the envelopes inside, from Yong Myung."

"You did?"

Tony nodded. "I told you this was too dangerous for a P.I."

"That's how you found me?"

"Yeah. That place was horrifying, Max."

"They were shipping dog organs, weren't they?"

Tony nodded. "To Maine. And other secret clinics."

"The one here in Seattle?"

"There was one here?"

"Yeah. Didn't you find it?"

"There wasn't one listed."

Wasn't one listed? What about Helen and...?"

"Tony?"

"Yeah?"

"Where's Helen?"

"Who?"

"Helen. Martina. The blond?"

"Oh, her." Tony covered his eyes.

"Tony, did she make it?"

Tony nodded reluctantly.

"She knew something about Jenny. She—we talked. Where is she?"

Tony shook his head. "Gone Max."

"What do you mean? Where is she? I need to talk to her."

"She's gone Max."

"Gone?"

"As soon as she was stable, Federal Marshall's picked her up."

"What?"

"Witness protection."

"What the fuck?"

Max tried to sit up. The monitor at the side of the bed beeped furiously.

"Calm down Max."

"She knew something Tony. She said—she told me--"
Max stopped talking and closed his eyes against sobs he
knew would come.

"What did she say Max?"

"She said they killed her. That's what she said. Jenny's
dead."

"She's gone. There's not a thing we can do."

"We can find her."

"In wit-sec? Are you serious? Think, Max."

"Tony, her identity appeared three years ago, the day after
Jenny disappeared. She knows something. She knows who
killed Jenny."

"Max, it might be a coincidence."

"It isn't, Tony. It isn't!"

A nurse appeared. "You need to relax, Mr. Boucher. Lay
back."

"I said call me Max!" he shouted. "Use my fucking
name."

His shoulder was on fire. His right leg felt like it might
burn off.

"Max, chill." Tony patted his hand.

"You gotta find her Tony," he said.

The nurse prepared another syringe.

"I'll see what I can do," Tony said.

But even as the taste of metal intensified, and his eyes got
too heavy to keep open, Max knew it was hopeless.

Helen, or whatever her name was, was gone. The same as
Jenny. Either way, the answers he wanted were miles away,
and he had no idea where they might be.

When he woke again, his cheeks were wet.

And Tony was gone.

Max Boucher was all alone.

HARVESTED

Chapter Twenty-Eight

Max revved the Skylark's motor.

The sound invigorated him.

It was clean, inside and out. Eddie had given him a killer deal, grateful his dog had been found, returned, and was okay.

He'd gone over to Fran's diner while they finished the detail work. She hadn't minded that he brought his own dog, the rescued blue heeler. They hadn't been able to find his owner.

His name was Russ, and he needed walking and a trip to the dog park every day. Max needed the exercise too.

He carried a cane. Still used it from time to time, especially near the end of the day when he was tired.

But after six months, he was making his way back to normal. Whatever that meant.

His right shoulder still ached, but with regular visits to the gym, it was improving.

Leaving the parking lot, he turned right onto the main road, then down at the light took a left, petting Russ on the head as he drove.

"Just one little stop buddy, and then we'll head to the apartment." He still couldn't bring himself to call that place home.

Several blocks later, took another left. Pulled up in front of the house.

His house, in Queen Anne. There was a new sign on the lawn.

The inside had been cleaned and staged for the sale. Next week, he would have to spend some time here and removing anything personal he wanted to keep before the new buyers took possession. Max sat out front, looking at the yard. The door. The bushes out front.

He touched the wedding ring on his finger, and for the first time in years he slid it off and into his jacket pocket. His eyes filled with tears.

He'd had one last look around the house over the last few months. Several, if he was honest with himself. But there was nothing new.

He'd sold Jenny's car finally. The garage was empty now.

Finally, last week, he agreed to put the place on the market. He priced it to sell, and offers poured in. He'd screened the potential purchasers, found a family, a mother and father with a daughter and a dog. A mutt to be exact. Max liked them. Their offer was not the highest, but it was the one he accepted.

He looked at the realtor's sign, with the "Sold" moniker on the top. He'd just go in for one second.

"C'mon Russ," he said.

The dog leaped out of the car on his side and nearly knocked him to the ground. Max stumbled and then laughed, feeling a sense of relief as he reached into his pocket and hit the garage door opener he still had there. Russ ran into the garage and Max limped after him.

Suddenly things felt odd. Max hadn't spent much time in the garage, as the assumption had been that nothing happened in here on the night his family had disappeared. Besides, Jenny's car had been in the way.

On the floor in the center of the driveway, directly under where the car had been parked were several rust-red drops. Russ went straight to the area but sat down next to them and whined. Max got closer and realized it was dried blood.

The blood rushed to his head and he nearly fainted. His heart pounded. Had Jenny's car really been covering a clue he'd missed this whole time?

Russ barked, and that brought him back to reality. Max took out his phone and took a few pictures from different angles.

Then he pulled up Tony's contact information but hesitated over the call button. He wanted help, the cops, the best forensics team, but he wouldn't get it for a cold case like this one. There would be so many questions, and they had given up so quickly before. No, Max would do this his way.

He'd have to call the realtor in the morning, back out of the deal. He couldn't possibly sell the house now.

Helen had said his wife was dead, and that felt true, although he'd like some more answers about what happened.

But it also meant Jenny's killer or killers were still out there, and Max intended to catch whoever they were.

Max leaned against the wall and slid heavily to the floor simply staring at the blood spots. Russ came over and put his head on Max's lap.

"We'll figure this out boy," Max said. "We'll figure it out together."

With an effort he stood and walked toward the door that led into the house. "C'mon Russ," he said. "Let's go home."

He hit the garage button again, and the door slid slowly shut.

The End

About the Author

Troy Lambert is a freelance writer and mystery suspense author from Boise, Idaho where he lives with the love of his life and some very talented dogs. When he is not staring at a screen plagiarizing the alphabet, he can be found outside, hiking, camping, riding his bike, skiing, or generally enjoying the outdoors. You can find his other work on his Amazon author page.

If you enjoyed this book, you might also enjoy *Stray Ally*, a book about a man who finds a dog in the wilderness and saves him. In the end, the dog proves to be truly the man's Stray Ally, proving that dogs are indeed man's best friend. https://www.amazon.com/Stray-Ally-Troy-Lambert-ebook/dp/B00IRFVC98

CPSIA information can be obtained
at www.ICGtesting.com
Printed in the USA
BVHW031521180619
551189BV00046B/684/P